William Howard Doane

The Silver Spray

William Howard Doane

The Silver Spray

ISBN/EAN: 9783337334864

Printed in Europe, USA, Canada, Australia, Japan

Cover: Foto ©Andreas Hilbeck / pixelio.de

More available books at **www.hansebooks.com**

THE SILVER SPRAY;

A NEW AND CHOICE COLLECTION OF

Popular Sabbath-School Music,

CONSISTING OF

Duets, Quartets, Chants, Choruses, &c.

ADAPTED FOR

ANNIVERSARY MEETINGS,

SABBATH-SCHOOL AND TEMPERANCE CELEBRATIONS,

HOME AND SOCIAL CIRCLE, ETC

BY

W. H. DOANE.

CINCINNATI:

PUBLISHED BY JOHN CHURCH & CO., 66 W. FOURTH ST.

THE SILVER SPRAY.

LEAD THEM TO THEE.

Rev. R. Lowry.

1. Lead them, my God, to thee, Lead them to thee, These chil-dren
2. When earth looks bright and fair, Fes - - tive and gay, Let no de-

dear of mine, Thou gav-est me, O, by thy love di - vine,
lu - sive snare, Lure them a-stray; But from tempt-a - tion's power,

Lead them, my God, to thee, Lead them, Lead them, Lead them to thee.
Lead them, my God, to thee, Lead them, Lead them, Lead them to thee.

3 E'en for such little ones,
　Christ came a child,
And thro' this world of sin,
　Moved undefiled;
O, for his sake, I pray,
Lead them, my God, to thee,
　Lead them to thee.

4 Yea, tho' my faith be dim,
　I would believe
That thou this precious gift,
　Wilt now receive;
O, take their young hearts now;
Lead them, my God, to thee,
　Lead them to thee.

SOLDIERS FOR JESUS.

W. H. DOANE.

With Spirit.

1. On - ward, press on - ward, the great com-mand, Who'll be the first to the first to

2. What have we done in the week that's past? What if this hour should

join our band? Who from the snares of the world will fly, And

be our last? Have we been seek - ing, with earn - est heart, To

Chorus.

prove the joys that will nev - er die? Sol - diers for Je - sus,

choose, like Ma - ry, the bet - ter part? Sol - diers, etc.

Sol - diers for Je - sus, Sol - diers for Je - sus we will be;

Sol-diers for Je - sus, Sol - diers for Je - sus, Sol-diers for Je - sus we will be.

3 Onward, still onward, our way pursue,
   Working with zeal and courage, too,
   Bearing with patience the ills we meet—
   'T is grief that makes every joy more sweet.
   Soldiers for Jesus, etc.

IF I COME TO JESUS.

(Infant Class Song.)

"Suffer little ones to come unto me."

W. H. DOANE.

1. If I come to Je-sus, He will make me glad;
2. If I come to Je-sus, He will hear my prayer;

He will give me pleas-ure, When my heart is sad.
He will love me dear-ly— He my sins did bear.

Chorus.

If I come to Je-sus, Hap-py I should be,

He is gent-ly call-ing Lit-tle ones like me.

3 If I come to Jesus,
   He will take my hand
   He will kindly lead me
   To a better land.
      If I come, etc.

4 There with happy children,
   Robed in snowy white,
   I shall see my Savior,
   In that world so bright.
      If I come, etc.

RESTING BY AND BY.

"Let us labor therefore to enter into that rest."—HEB. iv: 11.

Words by Rev. SYDNEY DYER.   Music by Rev. R. LOWRY.

1. When, faint and weary toil-ing, The sweat drops on my brow, I long to rest from
There comes a gen - tle chid-ing, To quell each mourning sigh: "Work

2. This life to toil is giv - en, And he im-proves it best Who seeks by pa - tient
Then, pilgrim, worn and weary, Press on, the goal is nigh; The

la - bor, To drop the burden now— while the day is shining, There's resting by and by.

la - bor To en-ter in-to rest; prize is straight before thee, There's resting by and by.

Chorus.

Rest-ing by and by, There's rest-ing by and by, We shall not al - ways la-bor, We shall not always cry; The end is drawing nearer, The end for which we sigh; We'll lay our hea - vy bur - dens down—There's resting by and by.

3 Nor ask, when overburdened,
  You long for friendly aid,
  "Why idle stands my brother,
  No yoke upon him laid?"
  The Master bids him tarry,
  And dare you ask him why?
  "Go, labor in my vineyard,
  There's resting by and by."
    Resting, etc.

4 Wan reaper in the harvest,
  Let this thy strength sustain,
  Each sheaf that fills the garner
  Brings you eternal gain;
  Then bear the cross with patience,
  To fields of duty hie,
  'Tis sweet to work for Jesus,
  There's resting by and by.
    Resting, etc.

MY PRECIOUS BIBLE.

Words by Mrs. H. E. Brown.

W. H. Doane.

With Spirit.

1. My Bi-ble precious treasure! Worth more than gems of gold; Be it my choicest
treasure Thy cov-ers to un-fold. Thy fair il-lum-ined pa-ges With God's own glo-ry shine; Down thro' the long, long a-ges, It gleams in ev'-ry line.

2 For God's exceed-ing glo-ry, His ver-y life is love; All through his sacred
sto-ry Its splendor is in-wove. It glows in man's cre-a-tion, And O! more radiant still, In his complete sal-va-tion, From sin and mortal ill.

My pre-cious Bi-ble! 'tis a book divine, Where heavenly truth and mercy shine, And
wisdom speaks in ev'-ry line, Speaks to me, speaks to me, Speaks good news to me.

3 I read and weep and wonder
  How God, a holy God,
Could still the law's wild thunder,
  With mercy, gentle word.
How raise the pale transgressor,
  Bow low with pain and fear,
And make him heaven's possessor,
  With Christ, the Son, an Heir.
  My precious Bible, etc.

4 O, marvellous relation!
  O, tender, pitying love!
Of saints the admiration,
  The song of Host above.
Be this my wondrous story,
  My daily, fresh delight,
And in this flood of glory,
  My soul be ever bright.
  My precious Bible, etc.

JESUS BY THE SEA.

GEO. F. ROOT. By permission.

Reverentially.

1. O, I love to think of Je - sus as he sat be-side the sea, Where the
2. O, I love to think of Je - sus as he walked up-on the sea, When the
3. O, I love to think of Je - sus as he walked be-side the sea, Where the

waves were only murm'ring on the strand, When he sat with-in the boat, on the
waves were rolling fear-ful - ly and grand, How the winds and waves were still, at the
fishers spread their nets up - on the shore, How he bade them fol-low him, and for-

sil - ver wave a - float, While he taught the wait-ing peo - ple on the land.
bid - ding of his will, While he brought his loved dis - ci - ples safe to land.
sake the paths of sin, And to be his true dis - ci - ples ev - er - more.

Chorus.

O! I love to think of Je - sus by the sea; O! I
O! I love to think of Je - sus by the sea; O! I
O! I love to think of Je - sus by the sea; O! I

love to think of Je - sus by the sea, And I love the precious Word, Which he
love to think of Je - sus by the sea, How he walked up - on the wave, His lov-
love to think of Je - sus by the sea, And I long to leave my all, At the

spake to them that heard, While he taught the wait-ing peo - ple by the 'sea.
lov - ed ones to save, While he brought them safely o'er the storm-y sea.
dear Re - deem-er's call, And his true dis - ci - ple ev - er - more to be.

CHILDREN SING.

Words by FANNY CROSBY.

W. H. DOANE.

Sprightly, but not too fast.

1. Chil-dren sing, glad - ly sing, Hal - le - lu - jahs to our king; Lord of all,
2. Jour-ney on hand in hand, Sing-ing to the promised land, There is rest,

great and small, At his feet with rap - ture fall; Children sing, he is near,
there is rest, In the king-dom of the blest; Children sing, glad-ly sing,

Bending still his gracious ear, Trust in him: O, rejoice! Praise the Lord with heart and voice.
Till the heavenly arches ring, Till you hear the saints above, Praising God, for he is love.

Chorus.

Then sing, glad-ly sing, Sing, glad-ly sing, Till the heavenly arch-es ring,

Till you hear the saints a - bove, Praising God, for he is love.

3 Children sing, when the light
Wakes the rosy morning bright,
When the birds' tuneful lay,
Hail with joy the opening day.
Praise the Lord, he has made
Verdant lawn and forest shade.
Children sing, gladly sing,
Hallelujahs to our king.
Then sing, etc.

4 Children, sing! who can tell
If the song you love so well,
May not reach one whose heart
Longs to choose the better part?
Stealing soft, like the sigh
Of a zephyr passing by,
Children sing, ever sing,
Loudest praise to God our king.
Then sing, etc.

"STAND UP FOR JESUS."

Words by FANNY CROSBY.

W. H. DOANE.

Allegretto.

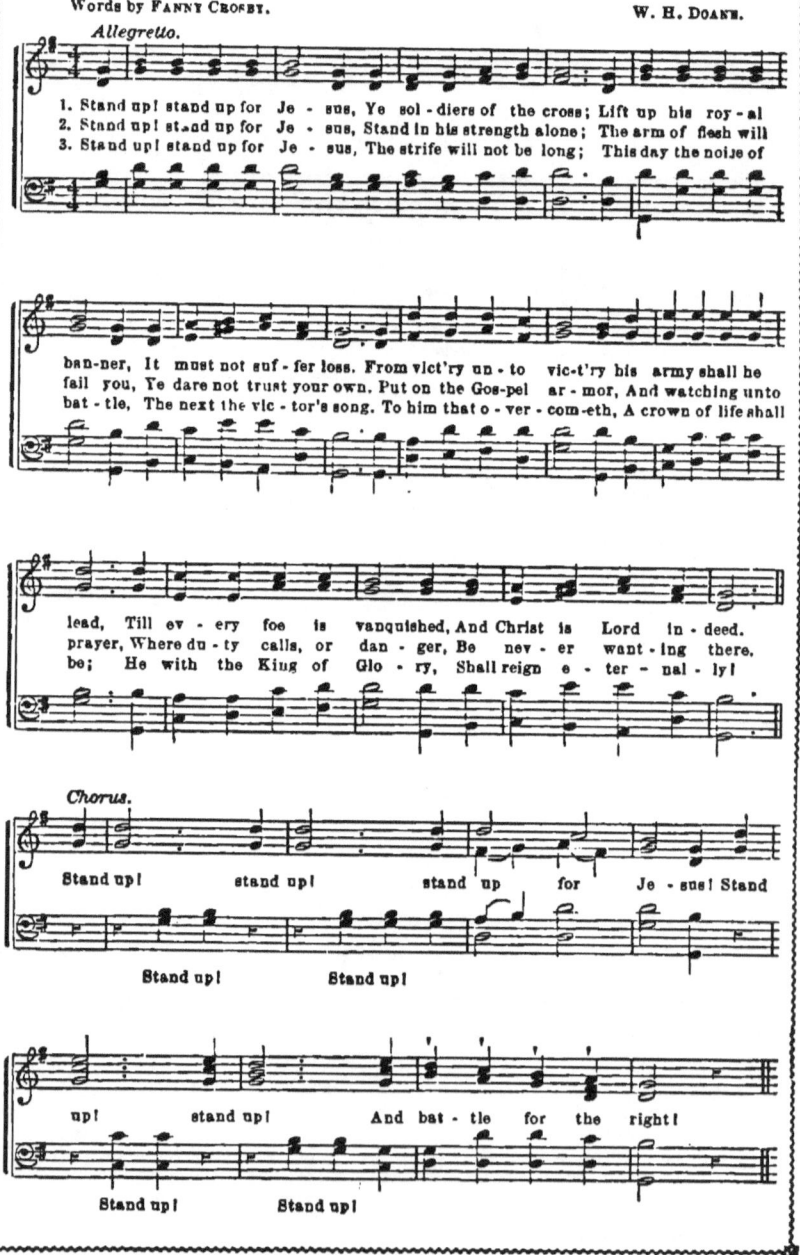

1. Stand up! stand up for Je - sus, Ye sol - diers of the cross; Lift up his roy - al
2. Stand up! stand up for Je - sus, Stand in his strength alone; The arm of flesh will
3. Stand up! stand up for Je - sus, The strife will not be long; This day the noise of

ban-ner, It must not suf - fer loss. From vict'ry un - to vic-t'ry his army shall he
fail you, Ye dare not trust your own. Put on the Gos-pel ar - mor, And watching unto
bat - tle, The next the vic - tor's song. To him that o - ver - com-eth, A crown of life shall

lead, Till ev - ery foe is vanquished, And Christ is Lord in - deed.
prayer, Where du - ty calls, or dan - ger, Be nev - er want - ing there.
be; He with the King of Glo - ry, Shall reign e - ter - nal - ly!

Chorus.

Stand up! stand up! stand up for Je - sus! Stand

Stand up! Stand up!

up! stand up! And bat - tle for the right!

Stand up! Stand up!

NONE BUT JESUS.

Rev. ROB'T LOWRY.

1. Weeping will not save me— Tho' my face were bathed in tears, That could not al-
2. Working will not save me— Purest deeds that I can do, Holiest thoughts and

3. Waiting will not save me— Helpless, guilty, lost I lie, In my ears is
4. Faith in Christ will save me— Let me trust thy weeping son, Trust the work that

lay my fears, Could not wash the sins of years; Weeping will not save me.
feelings too, Can not form my soul a-new; Working will not save me.

mercy's cry, If I wait I can but die; Waiting will not save me.
he has done, To his arms, Lord, help me run; Faith in Christ will save me.

Chorus.

Je-sus wept and died for me; Je-sus suf-fered on the tree;

Je-sus wept and died for me; Je-sus suf-fered on the tree;

Je-sus waits to make me free; He a-lone can save me!

Je-sus waits to make me free; He a-lone can save me!

THE PILGRIM'S JOURNEY.

"The Lord is gracious and full of compassion; slow to anger, and of great mercy."

Words by FANNY CROSBY.

W. H. DOANE.

1. Slow to an-ger, full of kind-ness, Rich in mer-cy, Lord, thou art,
2. Thou wilt nev-er, nev-er leave me, If I give my-self to thee,

Wash me in thy heal-ing foun-tain, Take a-way my sin-ful heart.
Teach, O! teach me how to praise thee, Tell me what my life should be.

Chorus.

I would go the pil-grim's jour-ney, On-ward to the prom-ised land;

I would reach the gold-en cit-y, There to join the an-gel band.

3 May thy ever gracious spirit,
  Lead me in the way of truth,
  May I learn the voice of wisdom,
  In the early days of youth.
    I would go, etc.

4 O! how sweet to rest confiding,
  On thy word that can not fail,
  Strong in thee, whate'er my trials,
  Through thy grace I must prevail.
    I would go, etc.

THE HEAVENLY LAND.

"Where the wicked cease from troubling, and the weary are at rest."

From Bradbury's "GOLDEN CENSER," by permission.

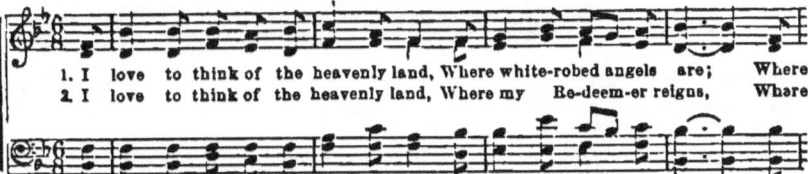

1. I love to think of the heavenly land, Where white-robed angels are; Where
2. I love to think of the heavenly land, Where my Re-deem-er reigns, Where

many a friend is gath-ered safe From fear, and toil, and care.
rap-turous songs of tri-umph rise, In end-less, joy-ous strains.

Chorus.

There 'll be no part-ing, There 'll be no part-ing,

There 'll be no part-ing, There 'll be no part-ing there.

3 I love to think of the heavenly land,
   The saints' eternal home,
Where palms, and robes, and crowns ne'er fade,
And all our joys are one.
   There 'll be no, etc.

4 I love to think of the heavenly land,
   The greetings there we 'll meet,
The harps—the songs forever ours--
The walks—the golden streets.
   There 'll be no, etc.

5 I love to think of the heavenly land,
   That promised land so fair,
O, how my raptured spirit longs,
To be forever there!
   There 'll be no, etc.

MARCHING ON!

Words and Music by Rev. R. LOWRY.

1. Marching on! marching on! glad as birds on the wing, Come the bright ranks of
2. Press-ing on! press-ing on! to the din of the fray, With the firm tread of
3. Fight-ing on! fight-ing on! in the midst of the strife, At the call of our
4. Sing-ing on! sing-ing on! from the bat-tle we come, Ev'-ry flag bears a

chil-dren from near and from far; Hap-py hearts, full of song, 'neath our
faith to the bat-tle we go; 'Mid the cheer-ing of an-gels, our
Cap-tain, we draw ev'-ry sword; We are bat-tling for God, we are
wreath, every sol-dier re-nown;" Heavenly an-gels are wait-ing to

ban-ners we bring, Lit-tle sol-diers of Zi-on pre-pared for the war.
ranks march a-way, With our flags point-ing ev-er right on t'wards the foe.
struggling for life, Let us strike ev'-ry reb-el that fights 'gainst the Lord.
wel-come us home, And the Sav-ior will give us a robe and a crown.

Chorus.

March-ing on! march-ing on! sound the bat-tle cry! sound the bat-tle cry!

For the Sav-ior is be-fore us, And for Him we draw the sword.

Marching on! march-ing on! shout the vic-to-ry! shout the vic-to-ry!

We will end the bat-tle sing-ing hal-le-lu-jahs to the Lord.

MORE LIKE JESUS.

Words by FANNIE CROSBY.

W. H. DOANE.

Slow, with feeling.

1. More like Je - sus would I be, Let my Sa - vior dwell with me; Fill my soul with peace and love—

D. S. Poor in spir - it would I be,

Make me gen - tle as a dove;

Let my Sa - vior dwell in me. More like Je - sus, while I go, Pil - grim in this world be - low;

FINE.

D. S.

2 If he hears the raven's cry,
If his ever-watchful eye
Marks the sparrows when they fall,
Surely he will hear my call.
He will teach me how to live,
All my sinful thoughts forgive;
Pure in heart I still would be—
Let my Savior dwell in me.

3 More like Jesus when I pray,
More like Jesus day by day,
May I rest me by his side,
Where the tranquil waters glide.
Born of him through grace renewed,
By his love my will subdued,
Rich in faith I still would be—
Let my Savior dwell in me.

16

ZION'S PILGRIM.

From "GOLDEN CHAIN," by permission.

Wm. B. Bradbury.

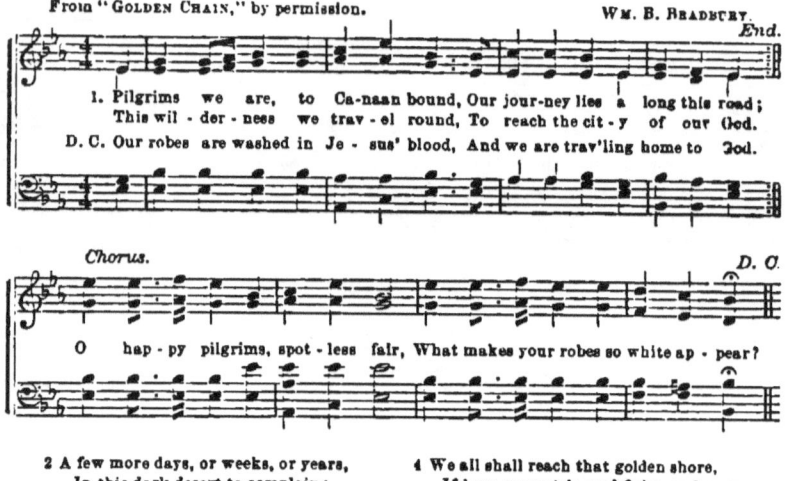

1. Pilgrims we are, to Ca-naan bound, Our jour-ney lies a long this road;
This wil - der - ness we trav - el round, To reach the cit - y of our God.
D. C. Our robes are washed in Je - sus' blood, And we are trav'ling home to God.

Chorus.

O hap-py pilgrims, spot - less fair, What makes your robes so white ap - pear?

2 A few more days, or weeks, or years,
In this dark desert to complain;
A few more sighs, a few more tears,
And we shall bid adieu to pain.
O! happy pilgrims, etc.

3 O, blessed land! O, happy land!
When shall we reach thy golden shore?
And one redeemed, unbroken band
United be for evermore.
O! happy pilgrims, etc.

4 We all shall reach that golden shore,
If here we watch, and fight, and pray:
Straight is the way, and straight the door
And none but pilgrims find the way.
O! happy pilgrims, etc.

5 O! may we meet at last above,
Amid the holy blood-washed throng,
And sing forever Jesus' love,
While saints and angels join the song.
O! happy pilgrims, etc.

I HAVE A HOME. L. M.*

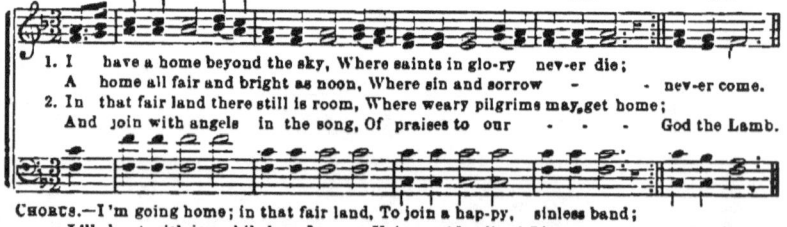

1. I have a home beyond the sky, Where saints in glo-ry nev-er die;
A home all fair and bright as noon, Where sin and sorrow - - nev-er come.
2. In that fair land there still is room, Where weary pilgrims may get home;
And join with angels in the song, Of praises to our - - - God the Lamb.

CHORUS.—I'm going home; in that fair land, To join a hap-py, sinless band;
I'll shout with joy while here I roam, Vain world, adieu! I'm - - - going home.

3 When done with earth, its follies past,
I'll reach my Fatherland at last;
To sit and sing around the throne,
"Glory to God! I'm safe at home."
I'm going home, etc.

4 When safe at home, in that fair land,
I'll join the happy, sinless band;
And sing with rapture near the throne,
"Vain world, adieu! I'm safe at home."
I'm going home, etc.

* May be sung as a duet and chorus.

A FRIEND THAT'S EVER NEAR.

From "GOLDEN CHAIN," by permission.   WM. B. BRADBURY.

1. Tho' the days are dark with trou - ble, And thy heart is filled with fear,
Cheer-ful hearts and smil - ing fa - ces Oft - en make thee hap - py here.

There is one that sees thee ev - er, And will hold thee near and dear.
Yet no one was e'er so hap - py, But sometimes the clouds ap-pear.

Chorus.

There's a friend that's ev - er near, Nev - er fear;

He is ev - er near, Nev - er, nev - er fear, There's a friend that's ev - er

Repeat pp

near, Nev - er fear, He is ev - er near, Nev - er fear.

All thy prospects will seem brighter
  When the shadow leaves the heart,
And the steps of time beat lighter,
  When the gloomy clouds depart.
Many days have dawned serenely,
  While the birds sang with delight;
But the skies were dark and gloomy
  Ere the sun had reached its height.
    There's a friend, etc.

3 Soon will dawn a brighter morning,
  On a blessed tranquil shore;
Sighs will then give place to singing,
  Tears to bliss for evermore.
Thou shalt see a world of glory,
  And eternal joy and bliss;
Let not then thy soul be moaning
  O'er the woes and cares of this.
    There's a friend, etc.

WHILE WE WORK FOR JESUS.

"Thou hast made me glad through thy works."

W. H. Doane.

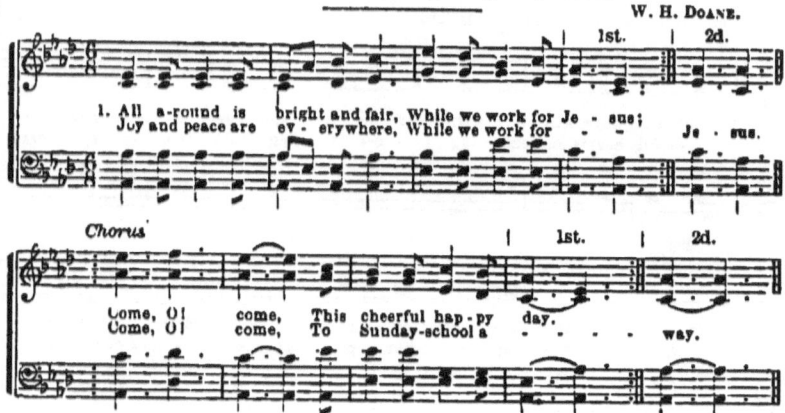

1. All a-round is bright and fair, While we work for Je - sus;
Joy and peace are ev - erywhere, While we work for Je - sus.

Chorus

Come, O! come, This cheerful hap-py day.
Come, O! come, To Sunday-school a - - - - way.

2 Every face with pleasure beams,
   While we work for Jesus;
Every heart with rapture teems,
   While we work for Jesus.
      Come, O! come, etc.

3 All the shades of sorrow fly,
   Clouds will never dim the sky,
Light and gladness shine around us,
   While we work for Jesus.
      Come, O! come, etc.

4 Nearer seem the realms above,
   While we work for Jesus;
Dearer seems our Savior's love,
   While we work for Jesus.
      Come, O! come, etc.

5 Let us raise a grateful voice,
   And with earnest hearts rejoice,
For the happiness around us,
   While we work for Jesus.
      Come, O! come, etc.

HASTE, O SINNER, TO BE WISE.

Arr. by W. H. Doane.

1. Haste, O sin - ner, to be wise, Stay not, stay not, for the morrow's sun!

Wis - dom warns thee from the skies, All the paths of death to shun.

2 Haste! and mercy now implore;
   Stay not for the morrow's sun!
Thy probation may be o'er,
   Ere this evening's work be done.

3 Haste! while yet thou canst be blest;
   Stay not for the morrow's sun!
Death may e'en thy soul arrest,
   Ere the morrow is begun.

TAKE A BLESSING WHILE WE LINGER.

W. H. DOANE.

1. Take a bless-ing, take a bless-ing, Ere we jour-ney on our way; Take a blessing while we lin-ger Where we long would gladly stay; 'T is the spir-it's ben-e-dic-tion, While the tear-drops free-ly start; Take the bless-ing, take the bless-ing, As it gushes from the heart, As it gush-es from the heart.

2. May the peace of heav-en ev-er At your hearth and board re-main; May the gentlest breez-es waft you O-ver life's un-cer-tain main. Take a bless-ing while we lin-ger, Where we long would glad-ly stay; Take the bless-ing, take the bless-ing, Ere we jour-ney on our way, Ere we jour-ney on our way.

3 Yes! these meetings and these partings
Will be over by and by.
When the loved and lost shall gather
At our Father's house on high;
Take a blessing, while we linger,
Where we long would gladly stay,
Take a blessing, take a blessing,
Ere we journey on our way.

CHRIST WAS BORN IN BETHLEHEM.

(Infant Class Song.)

Theme from THOMAS.

Arranged by W. H. DOANE.

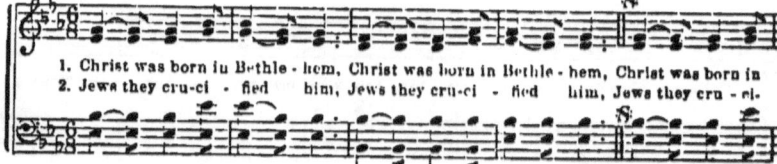

1. Christ was born in Bethle - hem, Christ was born in Bethle - hem, Christ was born in
2. Jews they cru-ci - fied him, Jews they cru-ci - fied him, Jews they cru-ci-

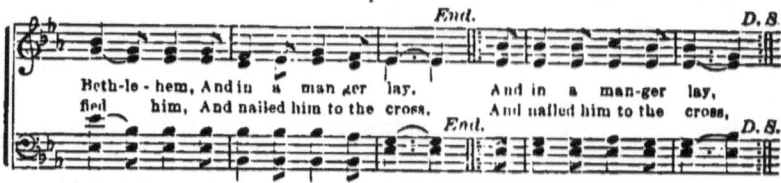

Beth-le - hem, And in a man-ger lay. And in a man-ger lay,
fied him, And nailed him to the cross. And nailed him to the cross,

3 Joseph begged the body,
   And laid it in the tomb.

4 Mary came a weeping,
   Her loving Lord to see.

5 Down came an angel,
   And rolled the stone away.

6 Shout, shout the victory,
   We're on our journey home.

COME TO JESUS EVEN NOW.

Words by MISS LYDIA BAXTER.

W. H. DOANE.

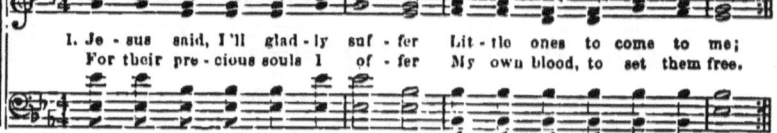

1. Je - sus said, I'll glad - ly suf - fer Lit - tle ones to come to me;
   For their pre - cious souls I of - fer My own blood, to set them free.

2. Once with lov - ing arms he held them Fold - ed in his fond embrace,
   And he said for such a kingdom Is pre - pared by heavenly grace.

Chorus.

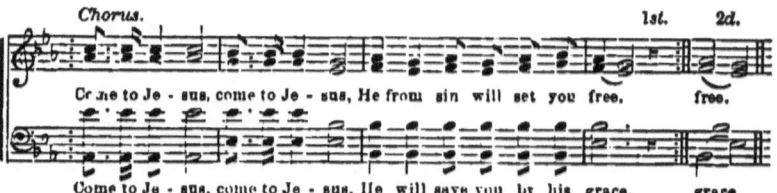

Come to Je - sus, come to Je - sus, He from sin will set you free. free.

Come to Je - sus, come to Je - sus, He will save you by his grace. grace.

3 Come, ere noon-tide sun effaces
   Morning's freshness from your brow;
Come, receive his warm embraces,
   Come to Jesus, even now.
     Come to Jesus, come to Jesus,
Come to Jesus, even now.

4 O! there'll be a glorious meeting,
   When the angels bid us come,
Through the pearly gates to greet him,
   In his bright, celestial home.
     Come to Jesus, come to Jesus,
Come, and heaven shall be your home.

DO THE RIGHT.

"No man, having put his hand to the plow, and looking back, is fit for the kingdom of God.

From "Singing Pilgrim," by permission.

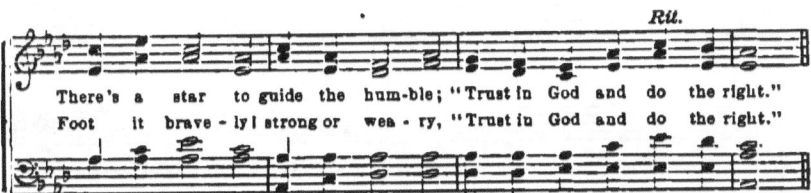

1. Cour-age, bro-ther, do not stum-ble, Though thy path be dark as night;
2. Let the road be rough and drea-ry, And its end far out of sight,

There's a star to guide the hum-ble; "Trust in God and do the right."
Foot it brave-ly! strong or wea-ry, "Trust in God and do the right."

Do the right, Do the right, "Trust in God and do the right."

Do the right, Do the right,

3 Perish policy and cunning!
Perish all that fears the light!
Whether losing, whether winning,
"Trust in God, and do the right."
Do the right, etc.

4 Trust no party, sect, or faction;
Trust no leaders in the fight:
But in ev'ry word and action,
"Trust in God, and do the right."
Do the right, etc.

5 Simple rule, and safest guiding,
Inward peace, and inward might,
Star upon our path abiding,
"Trust in God, and do the right."
Do the right, etc.

6 Some will hate thee, some will love thee,
Some will flatter, some will slight;
Cease from man, and look above thee,
"Trust in God, and do the right."
Do the right, etc.

COME, AND WELCOME.

"Suffer little children to come unto me."

Solt.   W. H. DOANE.

1. Come, and wel-come, to the Sa-vior; He in mer-cy bids thee come; Come, be hap-py in his fa-vor, Long-er from him do not roam.

Chorus.

Come, and wel-come, Come, and wel-come, Come to Je-sus, Come, O come. Come, and wel-come, Come, and wel-come, Come, and wel-come, Come, O come.

2 Come, and welcome—start for glory,
   Leave the wretched world behind;
   Christ will spread his banner o'er thee.
   Thou in him a friend shalt find
   Come, and welcome, etc.

3 Come, and welcome, do not linger,
   Make thy happy choice to-day;
   True, thou art a wretched sinner,
   But he 'll wash thy sins away.
   Come, and welcome, etc.

WE ARE GOING.

From "GOLDEN CENSER," by permission.

W. B. BRADBURY.

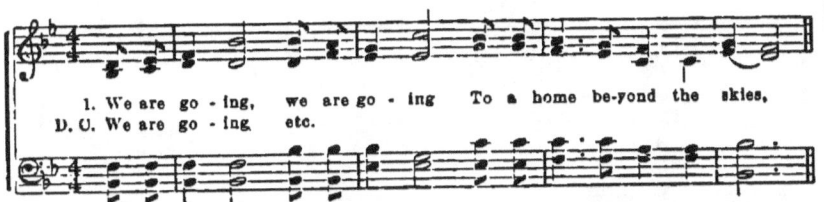

1. We are go - ing, we are go - ing To a home be-yond the skies,
D. C. We are go - ing, etc.

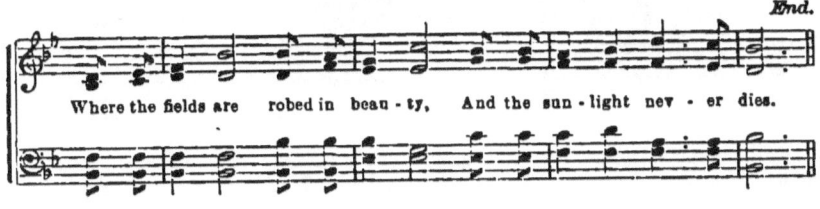

Where the fields are robed in beau - ty, And the sun - light nev - er dies.

End.

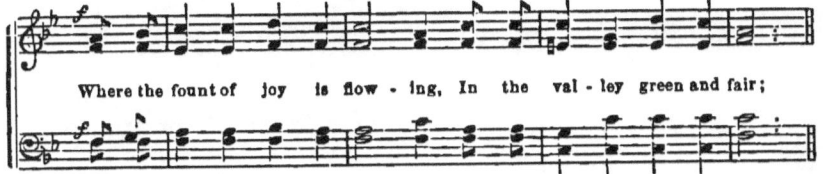

Where the fount of joy is flow - ing, In the val - ley green and fair;

We shall dwell in love to - geth - er— There will be no part - ing there.

D. C.

2 We are going, we are going,
    And the music we have heard,
Like the echo of the woodland,
    Or the carol of a bird;
With the rosy light of morning,
    On the calm and fragrant air,
Still it murmurs, softly murmurs.
    There will be no parting there.
        We are going, etc.

3 We are going, we are going,
    When the day of life is o'er;
To that pure and happy region
    Where our friends have gone before;
They are singing with the angels
    In that land so bright and fair;
We shall dwell with them forever—
    There will be no parting there.
        We are going, etc.

REST AT HOME.

Words by FANNY CROSBY.

J. HORN.

3 I want to be humble, resigned to thy will,
In sunshine or tempest to follow thee still,
Yet, lured by the tempter, how often I roam,
Forgetful, alas! of my God and my home.

4 No parent so tender, no friend is so dear,
No voice like my Savior's can banish my fear;
By faith in thy promise to thee I will come,
O, give me a place with thy people at home.

5 When shall I rise from this desert of gloom,
Beyond the deep shadows that darken the tomb,
In Eden, dear Eden, transported to roam,
And sing hallelujahs with angels at home?

DARE TO DO RIGHT.

From Bradbury's "GOLDEN CENSER," by permission.

1. Dare to do right! Dare to be true! You have a work that no
2. Dare to do right! Dare to be true! Oth-er men's fail-ures can
3. Dare to do right! Dare to be true! God, who cre-a-ted you

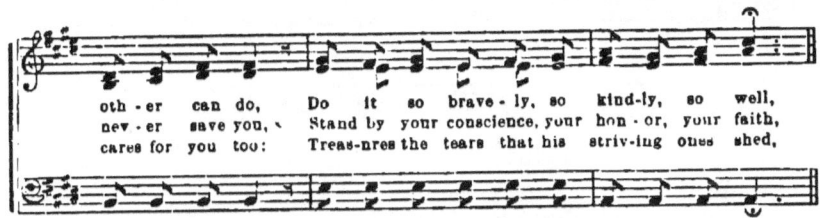

oth-er can do, Do it so brave-ly, so kind-ly, so well,
nev-er save you, Stand by your conscience, your hon-or, your faith,
cares for you too: Treas-ures the tears that his striv-ing ones shed,

Chorus.

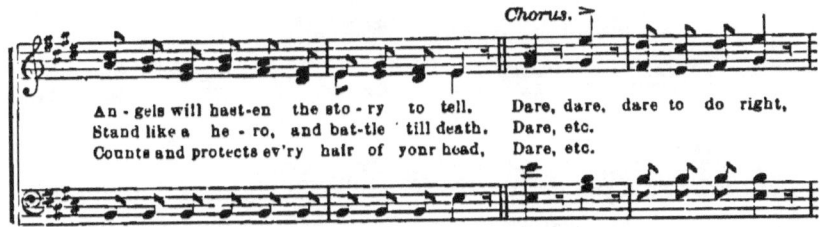

An-gels will hast-en the sto-ry to tell. Dare, dare, dare to do right,
Stand like a he-ro, and bat-tle till death. Dare, etc.
Counts and protects ev'ry hair of your head, Dare, etc.

Dare, dare, dare to be true, Dare to be true, Dare to be true!
Dare, .

Dare to do right! Dare to be true!
Keep the great judgment-seat always in view;
Look at your work as you'll look at it then—
Scanned by Jehovah, and angels and men.
    Dare, dare, etc.

5 Dare to do right! Dare to be true!
Jesus, your Savior, will carry you through;
City, and mansion, and throne all in sight,
Can you not dare to be true and do right?
    Dare, dare, etc.

BEAUTIFUL RIVER.

Rev. R. LOWRY.

1. Shall we gath-er at the riv - er, Where bright an-gel feet have trod,
2. On the mar-gin of the riv - er, Wash-ing up its sil - ver spray,

3 Ere we reach the shining riv - er, Lay we ev'-ry bur-den down;
4. At the smiling of the riv - er, Mir - ror of the Savior's face,
5. Soon we'll reach the sil-ver riv - er; Soon our pil-grim-age will cease;

With its crys-tal tide for - ev - er Flowing by the throne of God?
We will walk and worship ev - er, All the hap-py, gold - en day.

Grace our spir-its will de - liv - er, And pro - vide a robe and crown.
Saints whom death will never sev - er, Lift their songs of sav - ing grace.
Soon our hap-py hearts will quiv - er With the mel - o - dy of peace.

Chorus.

Yes, we'll gath-er at the riv - er, The beau-ti-ful, the beau-ti-ful riv - er,

Yes, we'll gath-er at the riv - er, The beau-ti-ful, the beau-ti-ful riv - er,

Gath-er with the saints at the riv - er That flows by the throne of God.

Gath-er with the saints at the riv - er That flows by the throne of God.

OVER ON THE OTHER SIDE.

Written, by request, for the THIRD PRESBYTERIAN SABBATH-SCHOOL, Cin'ti, O.

Words by Mrs. M. A. KIDDER.   W. H. DOANE.

"CLINGING TO THE ROCK."

W. H. DOANE.

Allegro.

1. When the tempest rages high, Sailing on life's boisterous sea; Stormy billows I de-

2. When 'mid drifting wrecks I'm cast, Darkness settling thickly round, Hope shall lift he
3. When the conquering waves shall close Proudly o'er me as I die; Over those brief victir

Chorus.

fy   If   I then may on - ly   be   Clinging to the Rock, Clinging to the Rock.

last,   If   I then be on - ly   found Clinging to the Rock, Clinging to the Rock.
foes,   I shal triumph while I   cry,   Clinging to the Rock, Clinging to the Rock.

Shel-ter for me ev-er, Strength that faileth never; When the storms of life are o'er,

Shel-ter for me ev-er, Strength that faileth never; When the storms of life are o'er,

Look for me on Canaan's shore,   Clinging to the Rock, Clinging to the Rock.

Look for me on Canaan's shore,   Clinging to the Rock, Clinging to the Rock.

THE HAPPY SUNDAY-SCHOOL.

Words from Bradbury's "GOLDEN CENSER," by permission.   Arr. by W. H. DOANE.

1. What do you do at the Sun-day-school? At the hap-py Sun-day-school?
What do you do at the Sun-day-school?

At the hap-py Sun-day-school? First we sing a song of praise,
Then we each our les-son say—

Then in prayer our voic-es raise; Clos-ing with an-oth-er lay.

Chorus.

That's what we do at the Sun-day-school, At the hap-py Sunday-school;

That's what we do at the Sunday-school, At the hap-py Sunday-school!

2 What do you learn at the Sunday-school?
  At the happy Sunday-school?
  What do you learn at the Sunday-school?
  At the happy Sunday-school?
  First, we learn commandments, ten—
  God's laws sent by him to men;
  Then what Christ did here below,
  To redeem our souls from woe—
      That's what we learn, etc.

3 Why do you love the Sunday-school?
  Love the happy Sunday-school?
  Why do you love the Sunday-school?
  Love the happy Sunday-school?
  There I with my Savior meet,
  At the blood-bought mercy-seat;
  Where he ever whispers, "Come
  To thy blissful, heavenly home—"
      That's why we love, etc.

WE ALL CAN DO SOMETHING FOR JESUS.

Words by FANNY CROSBY.

W. H. DOANE.

1. Our school is a vineyard, a garden of truth, Where all can do something for Jesus;
2. A word to the err-ing, of kindness and love, May often remind them of Je-sus;
3. Oh! sweeter, far sweeter than riches or fame, To feel we are working for Je-sus;

And though we are just in the morning of youth, We all can do something for Jesus;
D. S. A les-son, dear children, for you and for me, We all can do something for Jesus.

A song of our beauti-ful mansion a-bove, May lead a poor wanderer to Jesus;
D. S. A les-son, dear children, for you and for me, We all can do something for Jesus.

The cup of cold wa-ter we give in his name, Will bring us the blessing of Jesus;
D. S. No mat-ter how sim-ple the eff-ort may be, We all can do something for Jesus.

D. S.

The deep, roll-ing riv-er that flows to the sea Is made of the brooklet that sparkles so free;
The acorn, when planted, though small it may be, How quickly it grows to a wide-spreading tree;
The brook and the acorn, the leaf and the tree Are teaching a lesson to you and to me:

Chorus.

We all can do something for Je - sus, Some-thing some-thing,

We all can do something for Je - sus, Some-thing for Je - sus.

ANGELS ROLLED THE STONE AWAY.

Words by MRS. LYDIA BAXTER.

W. H. DOANE.

1. We're hap - py, dear Sa-vior, and shall we not sing, A song of thanksgiv - ing to
2. The grave could not hold him; on pinions of love The bright seraphs bore him in

Je - sus our King? We sought for his pres - ence thro' sor-row's dark way, And
tri - umph a - bove; A con - quering Savior heaven crowned him that day, For

D. S. We're hap-py in Je - sus, we're hap-py to - day, For

End. *Chorus.*

an - gels of glo - ry the stone rolled a - way. We're hap - py in Je - sus, we're
an - gels of glo - ry the stone rolled a - way. We're hap - py, etc.
an - gels of glo - ry the stone rolled a - way.

D. S.

hap - py to - day, For an - gels of glo - ry the stone rolled a - way.

3 Rejoicing in Jesus our union is sweet;
As heirs of his kingdom each other we greet;
Together we love him, together we pray,
For angels of glory the stone rolled away.
We're happy, etc.

4 We'll sing of salvation thro' Jesus the Lamb,
Till we on Mount Zion before him shall stand;
Forever with Jesus, forever to stay,
For angels of glory the stone rolled away.
We're happy etc

"THE SWEET EDEN SHORE."

Written for Fifth Presbyterian Sabbath School, Cin. O., H. W. Brown, Sup't.

Words by Mrs. M. A. Kidder.

W. H. Doane.

1. On the sweet Eden shore so peaceful and bright, The spirits made perfect are dwelling in light,
2. In that fair, peaceful land where Jesus is king, The song of redemption the glorified sing,
3. O, how blessed to rise when life's pangs are o'er, To mount up to heaven and dwell evermore,
4. On the sweet Eden shore, the home of the blest, With friends gone before soon we'll tarry and rest,

Their white wings are wafting them gently along, Thro' beautiful regions of glory and song.
And angels, too, join in the rapturous strain That the shepherds once sang on fair Judea's plain.
To never grow weary and never know care, In those beautiful regions so blooming and fair.
Contented with Jesus our Savior to stay, We'll drink of the joys that will ne'er fade away.

Chorus.

On the sweet E - den shore so peace - ful and bright,

On the sweet Eden shore on the sweet Eden shore

On the sweet E - den shore, the home of the blest, With friends gone before,

Eden shore on the sweet Eden shore,

We'll tar - ry and rest, tar - ry and rest, tar - ry and rest, with the blest.

NEVER BE AFRAID.

F c Bradbury's "GOLDEN CENSER," by permission.

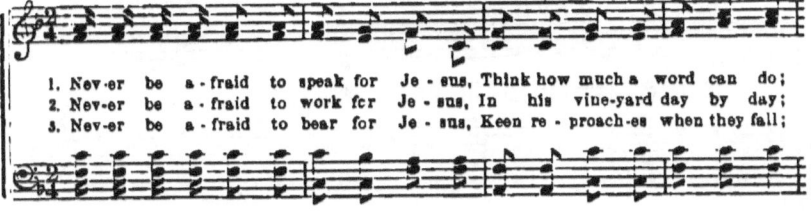

1. Nev-er be a-fraid to speak for Je-sus, Think how much a word can do;
2. Nev-er be a-fraid to work for Je-sus, In his vine-yard day by day;
3. Nev-er be a-fraid to bear for Je-sus, Keen re-proach-es when they fall;

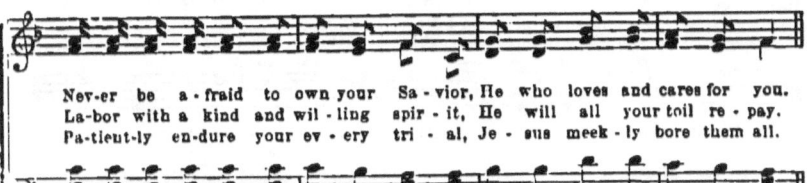

Nev-er be a-fraid to own your Sa-vior, He who loves and cares for you.
La-bor with a kind and wil-ling spir-it, He will all your toil re-pay.
Pa-tient-ly en-dure your ev-ery tri-al, Je-sus meek-ly bore them all.

Chorus.

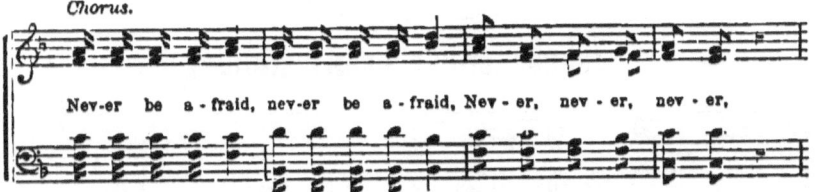

Nev-er be a-fraid, nev-er be a-fraid, Nev-er, nev-er, nev-er,

Je-sus is your lov-ing Sa-vior, There-fore nev-er be a-fraid.

4 Never be afraid to live for Jesus:
 If you on his care depend,
Safely shall you pass thro' every trial,
 He will bring you to the end.
  Never be afraid, etc.

5 Never be afraid to die for Jesus;
 He the life, the truth, the way,
Gently in his arms of love will bear you
 To the realms of endless day.
  Never be afraid, etc.

WAITING BY THE RIVER.

ARR. by W. H. DOANE.

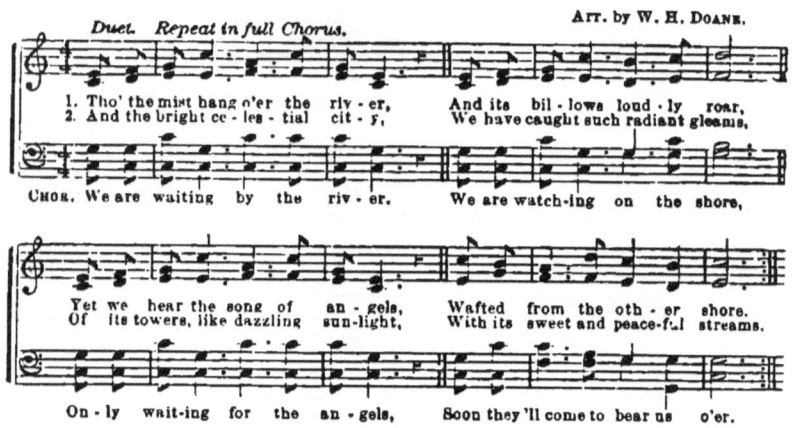

2 He has called for many a loved one,
We have seen them leave our side;
With our Savior we shall meet them,
When we too have crossed the tide.
We are waiting, etc.

4 When we 've passed that vale of shadows,
With its dark and chilling tide;
In that bright and glorious city
We shall evermore abide.
We are waiting, etc.

JESUS! LOVER OF MY SOUL.

2 Other refuge have I none—
Hangs my helpless soul on thee!
Leave, ah! leave me not alone!
Still support and comfort me.
All my trust on thee is stayed;
All my help from thee I bring,
Cover my defenseless head
With the shadow of thy wing.

3 Thou, O Christ, art all I want,
All and all in thee I find;
Raise the fallen, cheer the faint,
Heal the sick, and lead the blind,
Just and holy is thy name,
I am all unrighteousness;
Vile, and full of sin, I am,
Thou art full of truth and grace.

COME TO JESUS JUST NOW.

"Behold! now is the day of salvation!"

Rev. EDWARD PAYSON HAMMON says this was first sung in Scotland, when hundreds were asking, "What shall we do to be saved?"

With feeling and earnestness.

1. Come to Je - sus, come to Je - sus, Come to Je - sus, just

now, just now, Come to Je - sus, come to Je - sus, just now.

"Come unto me, all ye that labor and are heavy laden, and I will give you rest."—*Matt.* xi: 28.

1 Come to Jesus, just now, etc.

"Believe on the Lord Jesus Christ, and thou shalt be saved."—*Acts* xvi: 31.

2 He will save you, just now.

"God so loved the world that he gave his only-begotten Son, that whosoever believeth in him should not perish, but have everlasting life."—*John* iii: 16.

3 O, believe him, just now.

"He is able to save them to the uttermost that come unto God by him, seeing he ever liveth to make intercession for us."—*Heb.* vii: 25.

4 He is able, just now.

"The Lord is long-suffering to us-ward, not willing that any should perish, but that all should come to repentance."—*2 Pet.* iii: 9.

5 He is willing, just now.

"Him that cometh to me, I will in nowise cast out."—*John* vi: 37.

6 He'll receive you, just now.

"Flee from the wrath to come."—*Matt.* iii: 7.

7 Flee to Jesus, just now.

"Whosoever shall call on the name of the Lord shall be saved."—*Acts* ii: 21.

8 Call unto him, just now.

"And Jesus said unto him, Go thy way; thy faith hath made thee whole."—*Mark* x: 52.

9 He will hear you, just now.

"Jesus, thou son of David, have mercy on me."—*Mark* x: 47.

10 He'll have mercy, just now.

"If we confess our sins, he is faithful and just to forgive us our sins."—*1 John* i: 9.

11 He'll forgive you, just now.

"The blood of Jesus Christ, his Son, cleanseth us from all sin."—*1 John* i: 7.

12 He will cleanse you, just now.

"Therefore, if any man be in Christ, he is a new creature."—*2 Cor.* v: 17.

13 He'll renew you, just now.

"He that overcometh the same shall be clothed in white raiment."—*Rev.* iii: 5.

14 He will clothe you, just now.

"Greater love hath no man than this, that a man should lay down his life for his friends."—*John* xv: 13.

15 Jesus loves you, just now.

The Scripture pertaining to each verse should be read or recited by the Superintendent, in a plain and impressive manner, *before* singing the verse.

SABBATH BELLS.

From "GOLDEN PROMISE," by permission.   T. E. PERKINS.

Cheerful.

1. Come a - way, come a - way, Hark! the bells are ring-ing, 'Tis the ho - ly

Sabbath day, Pur-est pleasures bring - ing; Gold - en beams gent - ly fall,

Ev - ery thing re - joic - es, Lit-tle children, one and all, Tune their happy voices.

Chorus.

Come a - way, come a - way, Hark! the bells are ring - ing,

Sing a - loud, sing a - loud, Praise to God, our King.

2 Merry hearts, while they beat,
　Light our sunny features;
In the Sabbath-school we meet
　Friends and faithful teachers;
Kneeling there, kneeling there,
　Jesus deigns to hear us,
While we breathe our grateful prayer
　In our school so dear.

3 Happy place, happy place,
　O, the wondrous story,
Jesus died that we might live
　In the realms of glory;
Kindred hearts await us there,
　They have gone before us,
In that lovely mansion fair
　We shall part no more.

BLESS THIS HOUR OF PRAYER.

"Where two or three are gathered together in my name, there am I in the midst of them."

Words by FANNY CROSBY.

W. H. DOANE.

1. Come in our midst, O gra-cious Lord, Un-veil thy smil-ing face, Dis-
2. Come in our midst, O gra-cious Lord, Thy pro-mise we be-lieve, That

til in ev-ery wait-ing heart, The dew of heaven-ly grace; From
bids us seek and we shall find, Ask and we shall re-ceive; We

earth-ly scenes we turn a-side, On thee we cast our care; We
gath-er at thy mer-cy-seat, Our on-ly hope is there, We

wor-ship in thy ho-ly name; O! bless this hour of prayer.
plead the mer-its of thy blood; O! bless this hour of prayer.

3 Come in our midst, O gracious Lord,
    Eternal King of kings,
And fold the children of the law
    Beneath thy mighty wings;
Support the weak, the mourner cheer,
    Help all their cross to bear;
Thou Spring of Joy, thou Source of Life,
    O! bless this hour of prayer.

THE LION OF JUDAH.

Words and Theme by H. Q. WILSON.　　　　　　　　Composed by HENRY TUCKER.

DUET OR SEMI-CHORUS.

1. 'T was Je - sus, my Sa - vior, who died on the tree, To o - pen a
2. And when I was will - ing with all things to part, He gave me my
3. Though round me the storms of ad - ver - si - ty roll, And the waves of de-

INSTRUMENT.

fount-ain for sin - ners like me; His blood is that fount-ain which
boun-ty, his love in my heart; So now I am joined with the
struc-tion en - com - pass my soul, In vain this frail ves - sel the

par - don be - stows, And cleans - es the foul - est wher-ev - er it flows.
con - quer-ing band, Who are marching to glo - ry at Je - sus' com-mand.
tem-pest shall toss— My hopes rest se - cure on the blood of the cross.

Chorus.

For the Li - on of Ju - dah shall break ev' - ry chain, And

give us the vict - 'ry a - gain and a - gain.

4 And when the last trumpet of judgment shall sound,
　And wake all the nations that sleep in the ground,
　Then, when heaven and earth shall be melting away,
　I'll sing of the blood of the cross in that day.
　　　　For the Lion of Judah, etc.

5 And when with the ransomed by Jesus my head,
　From fountain to fountain I then shall be led;
　I'll fall at his feet, and his mercy adore,
　And sing of the blood of the cross evermore.
　　　　For the Lion of Judah, etc.

JESUS IS HERE.

"The Lord, whom ye seek, shall suddenly come to his temple."

Words by Mrs. Lydia Baxter.   W. H. Doane.

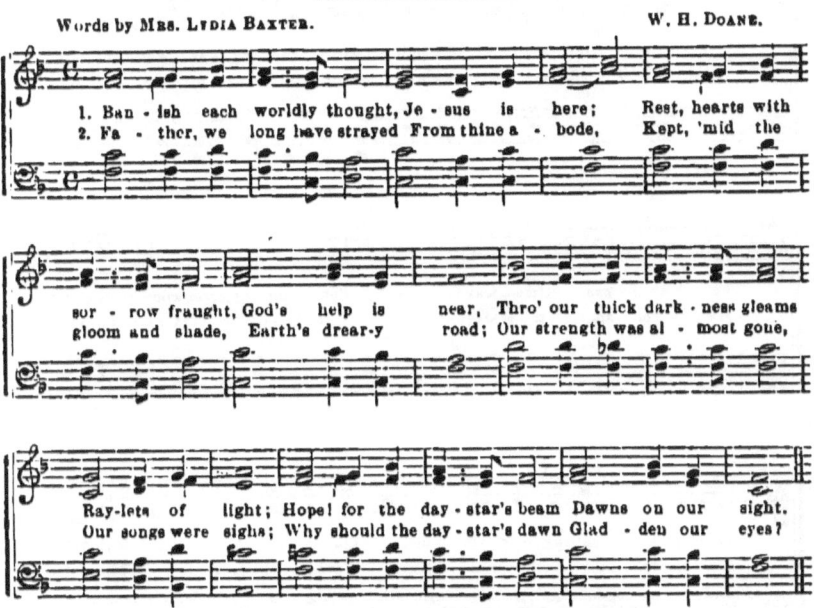

1. Ban - ish each worldly thought, Je - sus is here; Rest, hearts with
2. Fa - ther, we long have strayed From thine a - bode, Kept, 'mid the

sor - row fraught, God's help is near, Thro' our thick dark - ness gleams
gloom and shade, Earth's drear-y road; Our strength was al - most gone,

Ray-lets of light; Hope! for the day - star's beam Dawns on our sight.
Our songs were sighs; Why should the day - star's dawn Glad - den our eyes?

3 'T is of thy grace alone
Jesus is here;
Leaving his lofty throne
Our souls to cheer.
Hark! hear him whisper, Peace!
Every sad heart
Joys in the glad release
From sorrow's smart.

4 Hand clasped in hand we press
Upward to God;
On thro' the wilderness
Jesus has trod.
Peans of victory
Ring on the ear.
This shall our watchword be;
Jesus is here!

NEARER TO THEE. *6s & 4s.*

1 Nearer, my God, to thee,
Nearer to thee!
E'en though it be a cross
That raiseth me,
Still all my song shall be,
Nearer, my God, to thee,
Nearer to thee.

2 Tho' like a wanderer,
The sun gone down,
Darkness comes over me,
My rest a stone,
Yet in my dreams I 'd be,
Nearer, my God, to thee,
Nearer to thee!

3 Then let my way appear
Steps unto heaven;
All that thou sendest me
In mercy given;
Angels to beckon me,
Nearer, my God, to thee,
Nearer to thee.

4 Or, if on joyful wing,
Cleaving the sky,
Sun, moon, and stars forgot,
Upward I fly;
Still all my song shall be,
Nearer, my God, to thee,
Nearer to thee.

COME TO THE SABBATH-SCHOOL.

From "Golden Promise," by permission.

T. E. Perkins.

1. Beauti - ful child, with clust'ring hair, Twining the dai - sy white and fair,
2. Beauti - ful birds are on the wing, Beauti - ful songs of joy they sing,

Turn from thy pas - times, leave thy play, Come from thy greenwood home away;
Waking the soul to praise and love, Tell-ing of rest in heaven a-bove:

Ten-der - ly steal-ing o'er the dell, List to its call the Sab-bath bell.
Beau-ti - ful child, with eyes so blue, Watching the fountain's sparkling hue.

Chorus.

Trip-ping, trip-ping, light and free, Come to the Sab - bath-school with me.

3 Happy and bright the greenwood bowers,
Merry and sweet the birds and flowers,
Weary of all thou soon wilt be;
Come to the Sabbath-school with me.
Beautiful hymns to God we sing,
Joyfully there thy voice will ring.
Tripping, tripping, light and free,
Come to the Sabbath-school with me.

I AM THINKING OF HOME.

"In my Father's house are many mansions."—*John* xiv: 2.

Words by MARY F. KIRBY.

Rev. R. LOWRY.

Not too fast.

1. I am thinking of home, of my Father's house, Where the many bright mansions be!
2. I am thinking of home, of the loved ones there, Dearest friends who have gone before;
3. I am thinking of home; I am homesick now, And my spirit doth long to be

Of the cit-y whose streets are all covered with gold, Of its jas-per walls pure and
With whom we went down to the death-riv-er's side, And so sad-ly thought as we
In the far bet-ter land, where the saints ever sing Of the love of Christ, their Re-

fair to be-hold, Which the right-eous a-lone ev-er see.
watched by the tide, Of the thrice hap-py morn-ings of yore.
deem-er and King, And of mer-cy so cost-ly, so free.

Chorus.

O, home! sweet home! sweet home! I am thinking, and longing for home;

sweet home,

Beyond the pearly gate, Many mansions wait For the weary ones who journey home.

4 I am thinking of home! yes, of "home, sweet home;"
May we all in that home unite
With the white-covered throng, and exultingly raise
To the triune God, sweetest anthems of praise,
Singing glory, and honor, and might.

BATTLING FOR THE LORD.

"I must work the works of him that sent me, while it is day; the night cometh, when no man can work."

By permission

T. E. PERKINS.

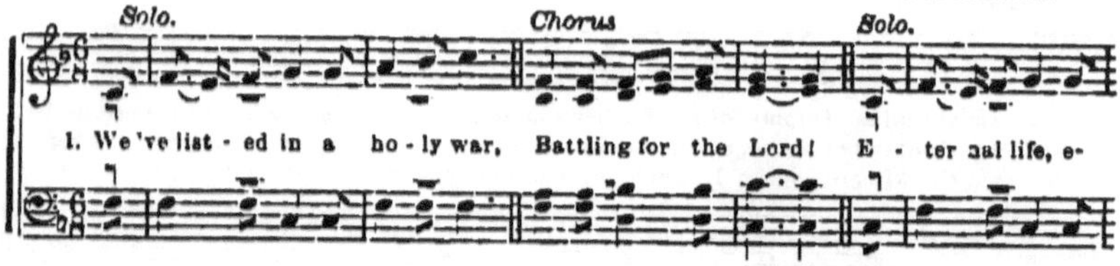

Solo.

1. We've list-ed in a ho-ly war, Battling for the Lord! E - ter-nal life, e-

Chorus.

Solo.

Chorus.

Full Chorus.

ter-nal joy, Battling for the Lord! We'll work till Je-sus comes, We'll

work till Je-sus comes, We'll work till Je-sus comes, And then we'll rest at home.

2 Under our Captain, Jesus Christ,
   Battling for the Lord!
   We've listed for this mortal life,
   Battling for the Lord!
   We'll work, etc.

3 We'll fight against the powers of sin,
   Battling for the Lord!
   In favor of our heavenly King.
   Battling for the Lord!
   We'll work, etc.

4 And when our warfare here is o'er,
   Battling for the Lord!
   This strife we'll leave, and war no more,
   Battling for the Lord!
   We'll work, etc.

5 Our friends and kindred there we'll meet,
   On the heavenly shore!
   And ground our arms at Jesus' feet,
   On the heavenly shore!
   We'll work, etc.

CODA, *for the last verse.*

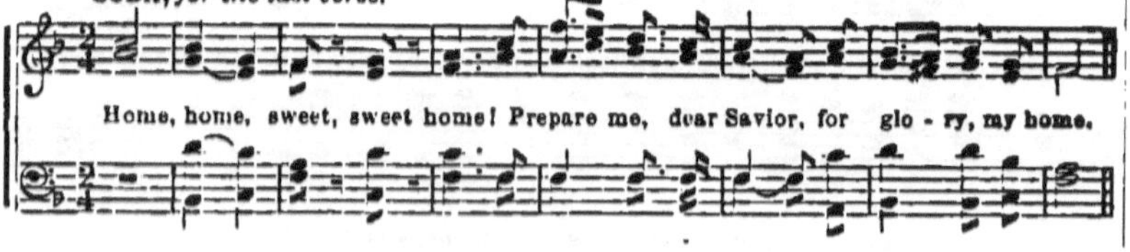

Home, home, sweet, sweet home! Prepare me, dear Savior, for glo-ry, my home.

RALLY FOR THE SCHOOL.

Words by FANNY CROSBY.   W. H. DOANE.

2 Come rally round our standard,
   A little pilgrim band;
   We are going home to Canaan,
   Our father's promised land;
   Come with us on our journey,
   And help us on our way,
   We long to see our number
   Increasing every day.
      Then rally, etc.

3 O, rally round our standard,
   For volunteers we call—
   O, rally round our standard,
   There is a place for all;
   Press on with zeal and courage,
   And when our work is o'er,
   A glowing crown awaits us,
   Of joy for evermore,
      Then rally, etc.

ANNIVERSARY HYMN.

Prepared expressly for the Anniversary exercises of the FIRST BAPTIST SAB-
BATH-SCHOOL, Cincinnati, O., Feb. 13, 1868.

Words by FANNY CROSBY.

W. H. DOANE.

1. An-oth-er hap-py, golden year Has brightly smiled and passed a-way;
With pastor, friends, and teachers dear, We hail our an-ni-ver-sary day!

Chorus.

Our welcome an-ni-ver-sary day, Our joy-ful an-ni-ver-sary day,
With pas-tor, friends, and teachers dear, We hail our an-ni-ver-sary day!

2 With grateful hearts to God above,
   We gladly join our festive lay;
   We thank him for the tender love
   That crowns our anniversary day.
      Our welcome, etc.

3 Our growing numbers still we view,
   With every week that glides away,
   While blessings fall like pearly dew,
   On this our anniversary day.
      Our welcome, etc.

4 Though some who once were with us here
   Have gone to fairer climes away,
   Perhaps their spirits, hovering near,
   Behold our anniversary day.
      Our welcome, etc.

5 And when these mortal scenes are past,
   When one by one they fade away,
   O! may we meet in heaven at last,
   To spend a long, eternal day.
      Our welcome, etc.

CHORUS OF FIRE.

Words and Music by Rev. R. Lowry.

1. O! gold-en Here-af-ter, Thine ev-ery bright raft-er Will shake in the
2. O! host with-out num-ber A-waked from death's slumber, Who walk in white
3. O! man-sions e-ter-nal, In fields ev-er ver-nal, A-wait-ing your
4. O! Je-sus, our Mas-ter, Com-mand to beat fast-er These weary life-

thun-der of sanc-ti-fied song; And ev-ery swift an-gel Pro-
robes on the em-e-rald shore, The glo-ry is o'er you, The
ten-ant-ry ran-somed from sin, We'll stand on your pave-ment, No
puls-es that bring us to thee, Till, past the dark por-tal, We

claim an e-van-gel, To sum-mon God's saints to the glo-ri-fied throng.
throne is be-fore you, And weep-ing will come to your spir-its no more.
more in en-slavement, With home-songs to Je-sus who welcomes us in.
stand up im-mor-tal, And sweep with ho-san-nas the jas-per-lit sea.

Chorus.

O! cho-rus of fire, That will burst from God's choir, When the loud hal-le-

lu-jahs leap up from the soul, Till the flowers on the hills, And the

waves in the rills, Shall trem-ble with joy in the mu-sic's deep roll.

O, YES! WE'LL BE THERE.

J. M. HOLMES.

Duet.

1. There is a beau-ti-ful world, Where saints and an-gels sing;
2. There is a beau-ti-ful world, Where sor-row nev-er comes;

A world where peace and pleasure reigns, And heavenly prais-es ring.
A world where tears shall ne-ver fall, In sighing for our home.

Chorus.

We'll be there, be there; O! yes, we'll be there.

Palms of vic-to-ry, crowns of glo-ry, We all shall wear;

We shall wear glo-ri-ous crowns In that beauti-ful world on high.

3 There is a beautiful world,
  Unseen to mortal sight,
And darkness never enters there—
  That home is fair and bright,
  We'll be there, etc.

4 There is a beautiful world,
  Of harmony and love;
O! may we safely enter there
  And dwell with God above.
  We'll be there, etc.

AM I A SOLDIER OF THE CROSS. C. M.

TUNE—ARLINGTON.

1 Am I a soldier of the cross,
  A follower of the Lamb?
And shall I fear to own his cause,
  Or blush to speak his name?

2 Shall I be carried to the skies,
  On flowery beds of ease,
While others fought to win the prize,
  And sailed through bloody seas?

3 Are there no foes for me to face?
  Must I not stem the flood?
Is this vain world a friend to grace,
  To help me on to God?

4 Sure I must fight, if I would reign:
  Increase my courage, Lord!
I'll bear the toil, endure the pain,
  Supported by thy word.

THE ARK OF GOD.

W. H. DOANE.

1. What ves-sel are you sail-ing in, While on the voyage of life?
Our ves-sel is the Ark of God, "The way, the truth, the life!"
D. C The night be-gins to wear a - way, We soon shall reach the shore.

And what's the port you're sail-ing for, What calm and peace-ful bay!

Tho port is New Je - ru - sa-lem, The realms of end - less day.

Chorus.

Then hoist the sails, Then hoist the sails, To catch the gale, Each sailor ply the oar,

2 Our compass is the "Word of God."
Our anchor steadfast hope;
The love of God fills every sail,
And faith's our anchor rope.
How many have you now on board
That noble ship divine?
Ten thousand thousand happy souls,
And room for all mankind.
Then hoist the sails, etc.

BEAUTIFUL LAND.

Words and Music by Rev. R. Lowry.

1. Je - ru - sa - lem, for-ev - er bright, Beauti - ful land of rest, No
2. Je - ru - sa - lem, for-ev - er free, Beauti - ful land of rest, The
3. Je - ru - sa - lem, for-ev - er dear, Beauti - ful land of rest, Thy

win - ter there, nor chill of night, Beau-ti - ful land of rest!
soul's sweet home of lib - er - ty, Beau-ti - ful land of rest!
pear-ly gates al - most ap - pear, Beau-ti - ful land of rest!

The drip-ping cloud is chased a - way, The sun breaks forth in end - less day! Je-
The gyves of sin the chains of woe, The ran-somed there will nev - er know!
And when we reach thy love - ly shore, We'll sing the song we've sung be - fore!

ru - sa - lem! The beau-ti - ful land of rest! Je-

ru - sa - lem! The beau-ti - ful land of rest!

Duet.   Ritard.

BEAUTIFUL LAND. Concluded.

Chorus.

We wait im-pa-tient to be-hold The gates of pearl, the streets of gold, And nes-tle safe in Je-sus' fold, In the beau-ti-ful land, The beau-ti-ful land of rest.

ANGELS HOVERING ROUND.

Arr. by W. H. DOANE.

1. There are an-gels hov'-ring round, There are an-gels hov'-ring round,
2. To car-ry the ti-dings home, To car-ry the ti-dings home,

There are an-gels, an-gels hov-'ring round,
To car-ry the ti-dings, ti-dings home.

3 To the new Jreusalem,
To the new Jerusalem,
To the new, the new Jerusalem.

5 And Jesus bids thee come,
And Jesus bids thee come,
And Jesus, Jesus bids thee come.

"GOLDEN GLEAMS."

Words by Mrs. M. A. KIDDER.

W. H. DOANE.

1. When I'm dreaming, sad-ly dreaming, Of the tri-als here be-low,
2. When I'm dreaming, soft-ly dreaming, Of the cit-y of the blest,
3. When I'm dreaming, sweetly dreaming, Of the pure ce-les-tial land;

Of the dark and sore tempta-tions, Ev-ery hu-man heart must know;
Where the wicked cease from troubling, And the wea-ry are at rest:
Of the crowns and spot-less garments, And the ho-ly an-gel band;

While I dread each surg-ing bil-low, As a-round my soul they foam,
While I hear sweet Cal-vary's sto-ry, Chanted on the heavenly hills,
When I near sweet heav-en's por-tal, O, what glo-ries meet my sight!

Gold-en gleams shine on my pil-low From the land with-out a storm,
Gold-en gleams from Je-sus' glo-ry, All my long-ing spir-it fills.
Gold-en gleams of joys im-mor-tal, Where King Je-sus is the light!

Chorus.

Heavenly cit-y, bles-sed man-sion, When I catch thy gold-en gleams,

How it soothes my ach-ing spir-it— How it gilds my earth-ly dreams!

THE LAND OF PROMISE.

From the "SUNDAY-SCHOOL BANNER," by permission.

Semi-Chorus.

1. Have you heard of the land of prom-ise, Far be-yond the glow-ing sky?
2. Je-sus dwells in the land of prom-ise, He who laid his crown a-side;

There is rest for the faint and wea-ry, There shall pleasure nev-er die.
Come to earth from his Fa-ther's kingdom, Wept and languished, bled and died.

Chorus.

{ Come, O come, and learn the sto-ry, }
{ Of the Chris-tian's home in glo-ry, } We are bound for the

land of prom-ise, Far be-yond the glow-ing sky, Hap-py home,

hap-py home, Hap-py home be-yond the sky.

3 Have ye heard of the heavenly Canaan,
  Where the good shall part no more?
Join our band, we are marching onward,
  Soon our journey will be o'er.
    Come, O come, etc.

4 Have ye heard of the holy city,
  Beauteous realm of joy untold?
Would ye roam by the shining river,
  Would ye tread the streets of gold?
    Come, O come, etc.

WHAT SHALL I DO WITH JESUS?

"What shall I do then with Jesus which is called Christ?"—MATT. xxvii. 22.

Words by S. D. PHELPS, D. D.   Music by Rev. R. LOWRY.

1. What shall I do with Je-sus, The Christ who may be mine?
Ac - cept him as my Sav-ior, Or .... spurn the gift divine?

His on-ly Son God gave me—I must, I do de-cide;
And Christ I take to save me, Or .... Christ is now de - nied.

Chorus.

"What shall I do with Je - sus?" I'll give my heart to Je - sus! Upon the tree on Cal - va - ry He gave his life for me.

2 What shall I do with Jesus,
   The precious Lamb of God?
I cast my soul upon him—
   He bathes it in his blood;
I'll gratefully confess him
   Before the vile and just;
My ransomed powers shall bless him,
   My sure and only trust.

3 What shall I do with Jesus?
   For him the cross I'll take;
All earthly losses suffer,
   Ere I the Lord forsake.
In scenes of joy and sighing,
   His love shall be the same;
While living and in dying
   I'll glory in his name.

4 What now I do with Jesus,
   When this brief life is past,
With me will be remembered
   Before his bar at last.
He will not then disown me
   With those who hate and scoff;
At his right hand he'll crown me—
   He will not cast me off.

"STAND BY THE RIGHT."

Words by FANNY CROSBY.

W. H. DOANE.

1. Working in the vineyard, Working all the day, Nev-er be dis-cour-aged,
2. Working for the Mas-ter, Do not be a-fraid, Tri-als may be-fall you,
3. Marching on to glo-ry, Still your way pur-sue, In your Fa-ther's kingdom,

On-ly watch and pray: Do your du-ty no-bly, Heart and hand u-nite,
Nev-er be dis-mayed, Put your trust in Je-sus, Keep your ar-mor bright.
There's a crown for you; Live for him who loves you, Keep your co-lors bright,

Minding the watchword, Stand by the right, Minding the watch-word, Stand by the right.

THY WILL BE DONE.

For the Death of a Teacher or Scholar.

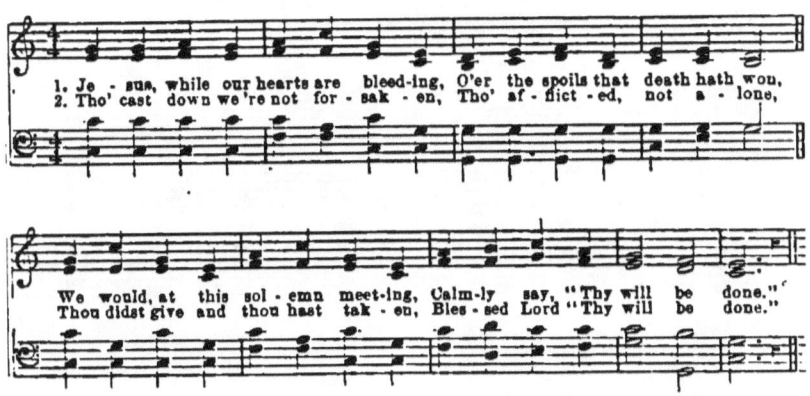

1. Je-sus, while our hearts are bleed-ing, O'er the spoils that death hath won,
2. Tho' cast down we're not for-sak-en, Tho' af-flict-ed, not a-lone,

We would, at this sol-emn meet-ing, Calm-ly say, "Thy will be done."
Thou didst give and thou hast tak-en, Bles-sed Lord "Thy will be done."

3 Tho' to-day we're filled with mourning,
Mercy still is on the throne;
With thy smiles of love returning,
We can sing, "Thy will be done,"

4 By thy hands the boon was given,
Thou hast taken but thine own;
Lord of earth, and God of heaven,
Evermore "Thy will be done."

BEAUTIFUL VALE OF REST.

Words by FANNY CROSBY.

W. H. DOANE.

3 The joys of earth, how soon they fade!
  Beautiful vale of rest;
  Like morning dew or evening shade;
  Beautiful vale of rest;
  Yet, when we reach thy golden strand,
  Our gentle Savior's promised land,
  We'll sing with all the angel band,
  Happy vale of rest.

4 O! who would dwell forever here,
  Beautiful vale of rest;
  With joy, unfading joy so near,
  Beautiful vale of rest;
  O! may I live that I may wear
  A starry crown forever there,
  And breathe thy sweet and balmy air,
  Happy vale of rest.

I WILL SING FOR JESUS.

"Singing and making melody in your heart to the Lord."

From the "Singing Pilgrim."

Philip Phillips.

1. I will sing for Je - sus, With his blood he bought me; And
2. Can there o - ver-take me An - y dark dis - as - ter,

all a - long my pil - grim way His lov - ing hand has brought me.
While I sing for Je - sus, My bless - ed, bless - ed Mas - ter?

Chorus.

O! help me sing for Je - sus, Help me tell the sto - ry Of

him who did re - deem us, The Lord of life and glo - ry.

3 I will sing for Jesus!
  His name alone prevailing,
  Shall be my sweetest music,
    When heart and flesh are failing.
      O! help me sing, etc.

4 Still I'll sing for Jesus!
  O! how will I adore him,
  Among the cloud of witnesses,
    Who cast their crowns before him.
      O! help me sing, etc.

OUR SAVIOR'S COMMAND.

"Knock and it shall be opened unto you."

From "SINGING PILGRIM," by permission.

A. J. VAIL.

1. O'er the por-tals of mer-cy these words are inscribed, And written in letters of gold;
2. O, ye wea-ry, draw nigh, 't is the place of repose; Ye footsore your journeyings cease;
3. All ye mourners, be-liev-ing, in con-fi-dence come; Ye des-o-late haste to look up;

The way-far-ing man may be-hold them a-far, And knock at the heav en-ly fold.
Ye toil-worn with la-bor, new vig-or put on, And knock at the port-als of peace.
Ye troubled in heart be re-signed to his word, And knock at the port-als of hope.

Chorus.

Knock, knock, knock, 't is the Savior's command, Knock at the por-tals a-bove;

Knock, knock, knock, 't is the Savior's command, Enter in-to the man-sion of love.

4 And ye sinners, O come! there 's a palace for you,
  Prepared by the Builder above;
  Approach with your burden, in meekness submit,
  And knock at the portals of love.
      Knock, knock, etc.

5 They 're all waiting within, and the feast is prepared,
  What folly to tarry and wait!
  Let every one come in obedient haste,
  And knock at the heavenly gate.
      Knock, knock, etc.

HEAR THE ECHO.

By permission.   T. E. PERKINS.

1. Ringing, sweetly ring-ing, The cheer-ful Sabbath bells, Ringing, sweetly ringing, The
2. Ringing, sweetly ring-ing, Their sil-ver chimes we love, Ringing, sweetly ringing, Their
3. Ringing, sweetly ring-ing, Those cheerful Sabbath bells, Ringing, sweetly ringing, Those

cheerful Sab-bath bells. We lin-ger a mo-ment their call to hear, Then
sil-ver chimes we love. A mis-sion of peace to the heart they bear, A
cheerful Sab-bath bells. O! let us be grate-ful to God a-bove, Who

haste a - way to our school so dear, O-ver the green-wood
wel-come call to the house of prayer, Tell-ing of rap-tures,
crowneth our days with the light of love, Bles-sed Re-deem-er,

joy-ous and free, Sing-ing with glad-ness hap-py are we.
tell-ing of rest, Man-sions of glo-ry, tran-quil and blest.
ev-er to thee, Praise from thy chil-dren of-fered shall be.

Chorus.   *mf*

While over the distant hill Their music is floating still, Hear the echo, ech-o, ech-o,

f   *mf*   *p*

sweet Sabbath bells, Hear the ech-o, ech-o, ech-o, sweet Sab-bath bells.

NOT WITH THE MULTITUDE.

"Great are thy tender mercies, O Lord."

Rev. R. Lowry.

1. It is not with the mul - ti - tude, I feel my heart re - vive;
It is not with the gid - dy throng. My soul is kept a - live;

'Tis in the si - lent, sa - cred hour, When none but God is near,

My heart is filled with sa - cred love, And rev - er - en - tial fear.

Chorus.

Not with the mul - ti - tude, Not with the mul - ti - tude,

No place is so sweet as the mer - cy - seat, When none but God is near.

2 It is not with the multitude,
   I hear the still, small voice,
Which whispers messages of love,
   And bids my heart rejoice;
O, no; 'tis when, withdrawn from earth
   And every earth-bound tie,
I hear thy kind, parental voice,
   And "Abba, Father," cry.

3 It is not with the multitude,
   My sweetest joys arise;
Nor even with the saints on earth,
   Though bound by sacred ties;
The fellowship of saints is sweet,
   But sweeter, better far,
Is fellowship with Christ, my Lord,
   The bright and Morning Star.

O, WE ARE VOLUNTEERS.

Geo. F. Root. By permission.

Not too fast.

1. O, we are vol-un-teers in the ar - my of the Lord, Forming in - to line at our
2. The glo-ry of our flag is the emblem of the dove, Gleaming are our swords from the

Captain's word; We are un - der marching or - ders to take the bat - tle field, And we'll
forge of love: We go forth, but not to bat - tle for earthly hon-ors vain, 'T is a

Chorus.

ne'er give o'er the fight till the foe shall yield.   Come and join the ar - my, the
bright immor-tal crown that we seek to gain.   Come, etc.

ar - my of the Lord, Je - sus is our Cap-tain, we ral - ly at his word;

Sharp will be the conflict with the powers of sin, But with such a leader, we are sure to win.

3 Our foes are in the field, pressing hard on every side,
　Envy, anger, hatred, with self and pride;
　They are cruel, fierce and strong, ever ready to attack;
　We must watch, and fight, and pray, if we'd drive them back.

4 O, glorious is the struggle in which we draw the sword,
　Glorious in the kingdom of Christ our Lord;
　It shall spread from sea to sea, it shall reach from shore to shore,
　And his people shall be blessed for evermore.

SACRED FOUNTAIN.

Inscribed to the YOUNG MEN'S CHRISTIAN ASSOCIATION.

Words by FANNIE CROSBY.   W. H. DOANE.

1. Thou whose hand did lead thy chosen people Through the desert on their pilgrim way.
2. Give us wa-ter from the Sa-cred Fountain, While we journey in a thirsty land;

In thy mercy grant us now thy bless-ing, Je-sus help us all to watch and pray.
Strong in thee no earthly foe can harm us, Thou our Rock on which we firm-ly stand.

Ritard.

CHORUS.

Father thou art pure and ho-ly, ho-ly, May our hearts thy tem-ple be,

Ritard.

O, make us humble, meek, and lowly, Poor in spirit, Savior, more like thee,

2 Gentle Savior, thou wilt never leave us,
Still from danger and from storm defend,
Sweet the promise to thy faithful children,
Thou wilt guide and keep them to the end.
Father, etc.

4 Though we pass the dark and rolling river,
Thou wilt bear us safely to the shore;
We shall praise thee in the vales of Eden,
With the saints and angels evermore.
Father, etc.

'TWILL NOT BE LONG.

Written, by request, for the Anniversary Exercises of the Second Baptist Church, Chicago, January 1, 1869.

Words by FANNY CROSBY.   W. H. DOANE.

Duet. Slow and gliding.

1. 'Twill not be long our jour-ney here, Each broken sigh and falling tear
2. 'Twill not be long the yearning heart May feel its ev-ery hope de-part,
3. Though sad we mark the closing eye, Of those beloved in days gone by,

Will soon be gone, and all will be   A cloudless sky, a waveless sea.
And grief be mingled with its song; We'll meet again, 'twill not be long.
Yet sweet in death their latest song— We'll meet again, 'twill not be long.

Refrain. Allegro.

Roll on,   dark stream,   We dread not thy foam;

Roll on, roll on, dark stream, roll on, We

The Pil - grim is long - ing for Home, sweet home.

4 These checkered wilds, with thorns o'erspread,
   Through which our way so oft is led—
   This march of time, if faith be strong,
   Will end in bliss, 'twill not be long.
      Roll on, etc.

"SO DO I."*

Words by Mary E. Stainburn.

W. H. Doane.

1. The Sunday-school is my delight, O, let us has-ten there, O, let us has-ten there;
'T is there we learn the way that 's right, And hear the voice of prayer, etc.

2. When spring with many an op'ning flow'r And blossom decks the ground, etc.
When summer's sun and gentle shower, Spreads beauty all around, etc.

Solo. Girls. Boys. Solo. Girls.

I love the Sunday-school, So do I, So do I, I love the Sunday-school, So do I,

Boys. Solo.

O, I love the Sunday-school, Hap-py, hap-py Sunday-school;

So do I. Yes, yes, yes, yes, Yes, yes, yes, yes,

O, I love the Sunday-school, *All. Loud.*

Yes, yes, so do I, So do I, So do I, So do I.

3 And when the cold and chilly blast,
Shall steal away the flowers,
Shall steel away the flowers,
When winter's snow is falling fast,
This joy shall still be ours,
This joy shall still be ours.
I love, etc.

4 Yes; if the sweetest flowers abound,
Or earth is clothed in snow,
Or earth is clothed in snow,
In Sunday-school we will be found,
For there we love to go.
For there we love to go,
I love, etc.

* The solo should be sung by a little girl, and the accompaniment, or words "Yes," by the entire class or school very softly.

GENTLE SAVIOR, BLESS THE CHILDREN.

Rev. R. Lowry.

1. Gen-tle Sa-vior, bless the chil-dren, Gath-ered on this sa-cred
2. Thou hast spo-ken words of com-fort, "Let the chil-dren come to

day; May we feel thy pres-ence with us, While we
me;" Though our hearts are weak and sin-ful, We may

meet to sing and pray. Safe-ly through the week de-
bring them, Lord, to thee. Gen-tle Sa-vior, while we

part-ed, Thou hast kept us by thy grace, Now we
thank thee For this ho-ly Sab-bath day, Turn our

come with joy to praise thee, Come to seek our Fa-ther's face.
thoughts from earth-ly pleas-ure, Lead us in the shin-ing way.

3 Bless our school, increase its numbers;
　Every soul with rapture fill;
Give our teachers heavenly wisdom,
　In thy cause to labor still.
When the day of life is ended,
　Bear us on thy wings of love,
There to join the saints in glory,
　In our Father's home above.

TAKE MY HEART.

"Blessed are the pure in heart."

W. H. DOANE.

1. Take my heart, O Saviour! take it Make and keep it all thine own;
2. Father, make it pure and holy, Peaceful, kind, and far from strife,

Let thy spir-it melt and break it, Turn to flesh this heart of stone;
Turn-ing from the paths un-ho-ly, Of this vain and sin-ful life;

Heavenly Father, deign to mold it, In o-be-dience to thy will;
May the blood of Je-sus heal it, And its sins be all for-given;

And, as pass-ing years un-fold it, Keep it meek and child-like still.
Ho-ly Spir-it, take and seal it, Guide it in the path to heaven.

FAINT NOT, DROOP NOT. 8s & 7s.

1 Faint not, droop not, weary pilgrim,
  In the faith of Jesus stand—
He will guard thee, and will guide thee
  Safely to the promised land.
What though thorns beset thy pathway,
  And the clouds are dark and drear,
Sing aloud the songs of Zion,
  For the port of peace is near.

2 Fear not though the billows threaten,
  God will send his angels down;
In their hands they'll bear thee upward,
  To receive the shining crown.
Faint not, droop not, weary pilgrim,
  Soon you'll join that happy band;
Through death's portals soon you'll en er,
  Safely to the promised land.

GO AND TELL JESUS.

"And they went and told Jesus."

By permission.   T. F. SEWARD.

2 Go and tell Jesus, when your sins arise
   Like mountains of deep guilt before your eyes;
   His blood was spilt, his precious life he gave,
   That mercy, peace, and pardon you might have.

3 Go and tell Jesus, he'll dispel thy fears,
   Will calm thy doubts, and wipe away thy tears;
   He'll take thee in his arms, and on his breast
   Thou may'st be happy, and forever rest.

THE ANGELS IN THE AIR.

Rev. R. LOWRY.

1. When life's la - bor-song is sung, And the eb - on arch is sprung O'er the
2. Dark tho sha - dows in the vale, Fierce the howling of the gale, But the
3. Flood the heart with parting tears, Frost the head with pass-ing years, Min-gle

sha - ded couch of death so still; Then the Lord will light the scene With the
shin - ing ones are near our door; With our robes as bright as they, We will
want and woe to - geth - er here; But the Lord will lift the cloud, That en-

an - gels, star - ry sheen, As they wel - come us to Zi - on's hill.
tread the star - ry way, With the sha - dow and the storm no more.
wraps the shining crowd, And we'll nev - er know a sor - row there.

Chorus. Steady time.

We'll meet each oth - er there, Yes! we'll meet each oth - er there, With the

angels in the air; Yes! we'll meet each other there; We'll meet each other there, Yes! we'll

meet each oth - er there, With the an - gels, with the an-gels in the air.

THE OLD, OLD STORY.

W. H. DOANE.

1. Tell me the old, old sto-ry, Of un-seen things a-bove,
2. Tell me the sto-ry slow-ly, That I may take it in—

Of Je-sus and his glo-ry, Of Je-sus and his love.
For I am weak and wea-ry, And help-less and de-filed.

That won-der-ful re-demp-tion, God's rem-e-dy for sin,
The "ear-ly dew" of morn-ing Has passed a-way at noon.

Tell me the sto-ry sim-ply, As to a lit-tle child,
Tell me the sto-ry oft-en, For I for-get so soon!

Chorus.

Tell me the old, old sto-ry, Tell me the old, old sto-ry,

Tell me the old, old sto-ry, Of Je-sus and his love.

3 Tell me the story softly,
   With earnest tones, and grave;
Remember! I 'm the sinner
   Whom Jesus came to save.
Tell me that story always,
   If you would really be,
In any time of trouble,
   A comforter to me.

4 Tell me the same old story,
   When you have cause to fear
That this world's empty glory
   Is costing me too dear.
Yes, and when that world's glory
   Is dawning on my soul,
Tell me the old, old story.
   "Christ Jesus makes thee whole."

THE LAMBS OF THE UPPER FOLD.

From "CHAPEL GEMS," by permission.

1. 'Mid the pastures green of the bles-sed isles, Where nev-er is heat or cold,
2. There are ti - ny mounds where the hopes of earth, Were laid 'neath the tear-w-t mold,

Where the light of life is the Shepherd's smile, Are the Lambs of the Up - per Fold.
But the light that paled at the stricken hearth, Was joy to the Up - per Fold.

Duet.

Where the lil - ies blos-som in fade - less spring, And nev-er a heart grows old,
O! the white stone beareth a new name now, That nev-er on earth was told,

NOTE.—This Brace may be sung as a Duet if desired.

1st. 2d. *End.*

Where the glad new song is the song they sing, Are the Lambs of the Up - per Fold. Fold.
And the ten-der Shepherd doth guard with care, The Lambs of the Up - per Fold. Fold.

Duet. D. S.

Lambs of the Up - per Fold, Lambs of the Up - per Fold.
Lambs of the Up - per Fold, Lambs of the Up - per Fold.

ANGRY WORDS.

H. R. Palmer.

1. An-gry words! O, let them nev-er From the tongue un-bri-dled slip;
2. Love is much too pure and ho-ly; Friendship is too sa-cred far,
3. An-gry words are light-ly spo-ken; Bitterest thoughts are rash-ly stirred;

May the heart's best im-pulse ev-er Check them, ere they soil the lip.
For a mo-ment's reck-less fol-ly Thus to des-o-late and mar.
Brightest links of life are bro-ken By a sin-gle an-gry word.

Chorus.

"Love each other," "Love each other," 'T is thy Father's blest command,

"Love one an-oth-er," Thus saith the Savior, Children obey thy Father's blest command,

"Love each other," "Love each other," 'T is thy Father's blest command

"Love each other," "Love each other," 'T is his blest command.

"Love one an-oth-er," Thus saith the Sa-vior, Children o-bey his blest command.

"Love each other," "Love each other," 'T is his blest command.

JOY-BELLS.

Sunday-School Anniversary Song.

H. TUCKER.

Joyfully, rather quickly.

1. Joy-bells ring - ing, Chil - dren sing - ing, Fill the air with mu - sic sweet·
2. Joy-bells ring - ing, Chil - dren sing - ing, Hark! their voic - es loud and clear

Joc - und meas - ure, Guile-less pleas - ure, Make the chain of song com - plete.
Breaking o'er us, Like a cho - rus, From a pur - er, hap-pier sphere.

Chorus.

Joy - bells! joy-bells! Nev - er, nev - er cease your ring - ing; Chil-dren! chil - dren!

Very Soft.

Nev - er, nev - er cease your sing-ing; List, list, the song that swells,

Loud. *Soft.* *Very Loud.*

Joy - bells! joy - bells! List, list, the song that swells; Joy - bells! joy - bells!

3 Earth seems brighter,
  Hearts grow lighter,
As the jocund melody
  Charms our sadness
  Into gladness,
Pealing, pealing joyfully.
  —Joy-bells, etc.

4 Joy-bells nearer
  Sound, and clearer,
When the heart is free from care;
  Skies are cheering,
  And we 're hearing,
Joy-bells ringing every-where.
  Joy-bells, etc.

"MANSION OF LIGHT."

Written, by request, for the West Arch St. Pres. Sabbath-School, Phila.

DUET.   W. H. DOANE.

1. Oh, say have you heard of that mansion of light, Our Father has gone to prepare?
Where falls not a cloud or a shadow of night; They tell us no sorrow is . . there.
2. Oh, where is that cit-y whose portals of gold Are o-pen by night and by day?
The city whose splendor can never be told, Whose pleasures will never de - cay?

BOYS.

Oh, yes, we have heard of that mansion so bright, And free from all sorrow and care;
Our Savior, the Lamb, is the glo-ry and light, The . . . . .
'Tis yonder, where joy-ful our spir-its may fly, Beyond the bright planets that roll;
A-bove the clear arch of the blue e-ther sky, The . . . . .

chil-dren of Zi-on are there. 'Tis a home where the wea-ry may rest,
beau-ti-ful home of the soul. 'Tis a home, etc.

The beau-ti-ful home of the blest; Oh, come, we are bound for that

man-sion of light, The beau-ti-ful home of the blest.

WORK, FOR THE NIGHT IS COMING.

From "Song Garden," by permission of Mason Brothers.

1. Work, for the night is com - ing, Work thro' the morn-ing hours:
2. Work, for the night is com - ing, Work thro' the sun-ny noon;
3. Work, for the night is com - ing, Un - der the sun-set skies;

Work while the dew is spark - ling, Work 'mid springing flow'rs;
Fill bright - est hours with la - bor, Rest comes sure and soon.
While their bright tints are glow - ing, Work, for day - light flies.

cres.

Work when the day grows bright - er, Work in the glow - ing sun;
Give eve - ry fly - ing min - ute Something to keep in store;
Work till the last beam fad - eth, Fad - eth to shine no more;

Work, for the night is com - ing, When man's work is done.
Work, for the night is com - ing, When man works no more.
Work while the night is dark - 'ning, When man's work is o'er.

WE ARE MARCHING ON TO ZION.

W. H. DOANE.

Solo. *Duet.*

1. { We are march-ing on to Zi - on, We are marching on to
   { For the way is bright be - fore us, For the way is bright be-
2. { We must ral - ly round his stand-ard, We must ral - ly round his
   { But our Sav - ior will pro - tect us, But our Sav - ior will pro-

Semi-Chorus.

Zi - on, We are marching on to Zi - on, And our hearts are full of joy;
fore us, For the way is bright before us, In our Savior we are strong;
standard, We must rally round his standard, There are foes on every hand;
tect us, But our Sav-ior will pro-tect us, If we follow his command;

Trusting in his ho-ly word, We will fight the bat-tle of the Lord.
More than conq'rers we shall be, When from all our trials we are free.

Chorus.

Full of joy, full of joy, We shall sing the song of
full of joy, full of joy,

vic-to-ry; Full of joy, Full of joy, We shall sing in heav'n above.
full of joy, let us sing,

3 We shall never lack for wisdom,
  We shall never be afraid,
  If we cast our care on Jesus,
    If we look to him for aid;
  When the conflict here is past,
  He will take his children home at last.

4 When we reach the bank of Jordan,
  When we lay our armor down,
  We shall go and dwell with Jesus,
    And receive a glorious crown;
  There, on Zion's tranquil shore,
  Join the noble army gone before.

WE'LL DRINK NO MORE.

TEMPERANCE SONG.

"Look not thou upon the wine when it is red."

By permission.   Words by JOSEPH

1. We're growing stronger ev - ery day, And dai - ly we new pow
2. Till crys-tal fountains cease to flow; Till beaming stars re - fus

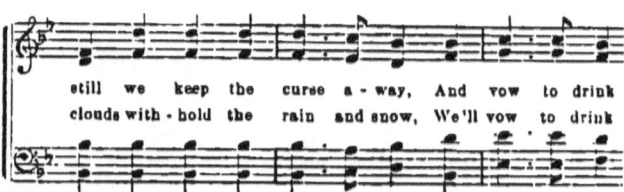

still   we   keep   the   curse a - way,   And   vow   to drink
clouds with - hold the   rain and snow,   We'll   vow   to drink

Chorus.

We'll drink no more of the rud - dy wine! We'll drink no more of the

think   to - day   of   the pledge we sign,   And   vow   to   drink

3 If Satan's power we thus withstand,
   And wide extend the Temp'rance band,
   'T will bring a blessing on the land,
   And men will drink no more!
      We'll drink, etc.

WHY DO THE ANGELS SING?

"There is joy in the presence of the angels of God."

Words by FANNY CROSBY.

W. H. DOANE.

Duet.

1. Why do the ho-ly angels sing? Why do the heavenly arches ring

With an-thems sweet from seraphs bright, With glitt'ring crowns and robes of white?

Chorus. *Rit.*

They sing of the Lamb that was slain, The Sa-vior that lives a - gain,

The root and the off-spring of Da - vid, The bright and morning star!

2 Glory to thee, our God, they cry,
 Maker of earth, and sea, and sky,
 To thee our highest strains belong,
 Thou great inspirer of our song.
  They sing, etc.

3 Beautiful world where all is bright,
 Rivers of gold and fields of light,
 In murmured tones of joy prolong
 The echo of the angels' song.
  They sing, etc.

4 Well may the holy angels sing,
 Well may the heavenly arches ring,
 With anthems sweet from choirs above,
 They sing of God, and God is love.
  They sing, etc.

"THE BATTLE CRY."

Written for HANSON PLACE BAPTIST SABBATH-SCHOOL

Words by Mrs. M. M. B. GOODWIN.

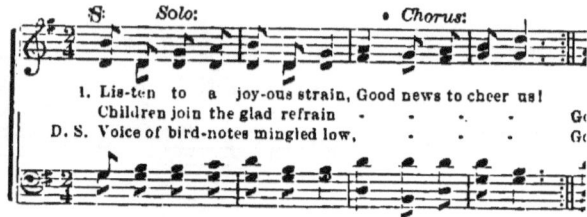

1. Lis-ten to a joy-ous strain, Good news to cheer us!
Children join the glad refrain - - - - G
D. S. Voice of bird-notes mingled low, - - - G

2. Sa-tan's cause's on the wane, Good news to cheer us
Je - sus shall the vic-to-ry gain, - - - - G
D. S. And our faith is true and tried, - - - G

Duet.

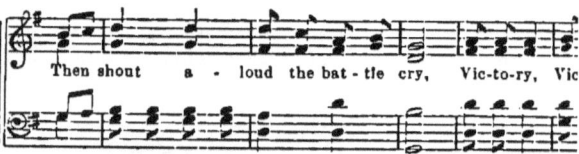

Sweet the mor - ning breez - es blow, Mur-m'ring streaml
Let it ech - o far and wide, We are on t

Chorus.

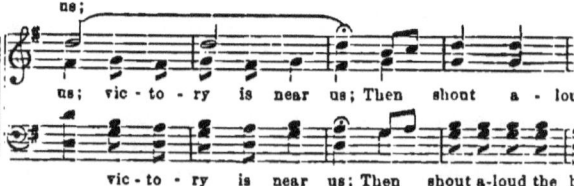

Then shout a - loud the bat - tle cry, Vic-to-ry, Vic
Shout a - loud the

ne;
us; vic - to - ry is near us; Then shout a - lou
vic - to - ry is near us; Then shout a-loud the b

Vic - to - ry, vic - to - ry Is near, is near

THERE'S SOMETHING I CAN DO.

Rev. R. Lowry.

1. A lit-tle child I am in-deed, And lit-tle do I know; Much
2. But e-ven now I ought to try To do what good I may, God

help and care I yet shall need, That I may wis-er grow—
nev-er meant that such as I Should on-ly live to play.

If I would ev-er hope to do Things good and great, and use-ful, too.
And talk and laugh, and eat and drink, And sleep and wake, and nev-er think.

Chorus.

There's something I can do, Night and morn-ing, Life a-dorn-ing,

Though I'm young and fee-ble too, There's some-thing I can do.

3 One gentle word that I may speak,
    Or one kind, loving deed,
May, tho' a trifle poor and weak,
    Prove like a tiny seed;
And who can tell what good may spring
From such a very little thing?

4 Then let me try, each day and hour,
    To act upon this plan—
What little good is in my power,
    To do it while I can;
If to be useful thus I try,
I may do better by and by.

"NO FRIEND LIKE JESUS."

Words by Mrs. M. A. KIDDER.

W. H. DOANE.

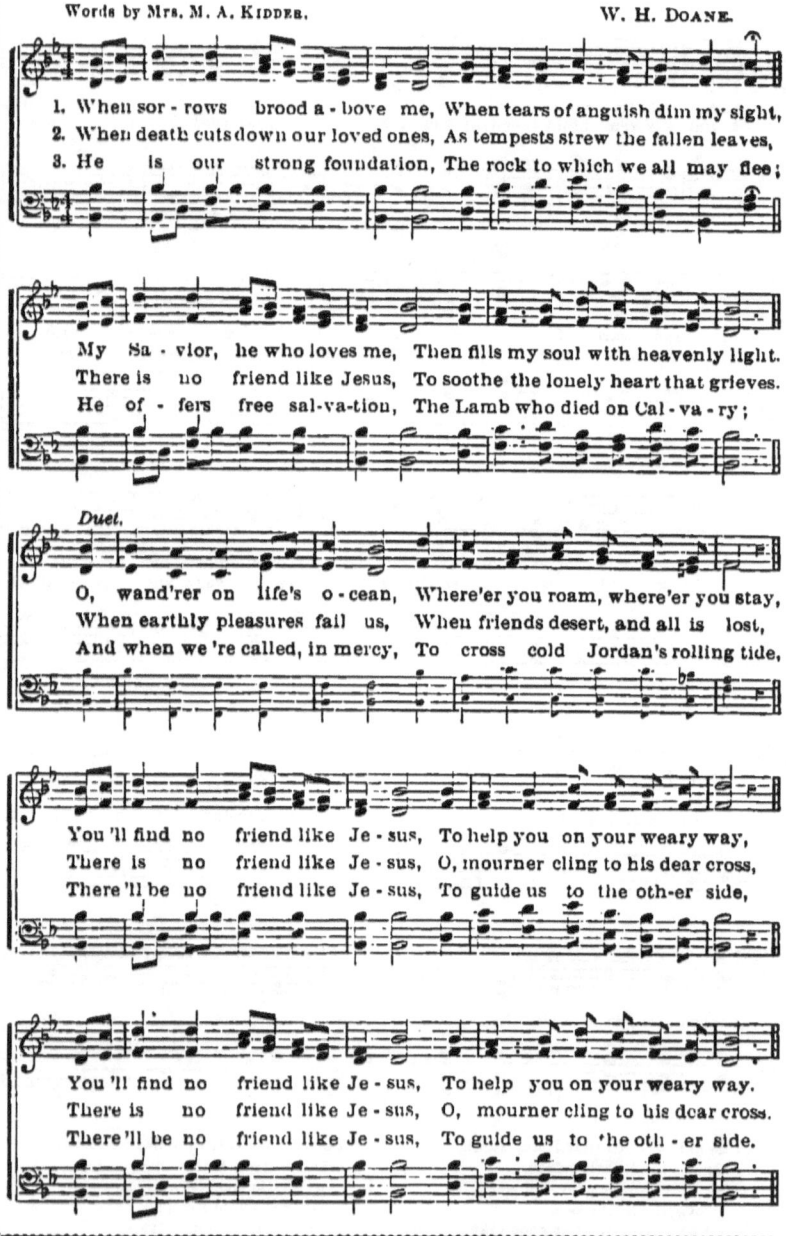

1. When sor-rows brood a-bove me, When tears of anguish dim my sight,
2. When death cuts down our loved ones, As tempests strew the fallen leaves,
3. He is our strong foundation, The rock to which we all may flee;

My Sa-vior, he who loves me, Then fills my soul with heavenly light.
There is no friend like Jesus, To soothe the lonely heart that grieves.
He of-fers free sal-va-tion, The Lamb who died on Cal-va-ry;

Duet.

O, wand'rer on life's o-cean, Where'er you roam, where'er you stay,
When earthly pleasures fail us, When friends desert, and all is lost,
And when we're called, in mercy, To cross cold Jordan's rolling tide,

You'll find no friend like Je-sus, To help you on your weary way,
There is no friend like Je-sus, O, mourner cling to his dear cross,
There'll be no friend like Je-sus, To guide us to the oth-er side,

You'll find no friend like Je-sus, To help you on your weary way.
There is no friend like Je-sus, O, mourner cling to his dear cross.
There'll be no friend like Je-sus, To guide us to the oth-er side.

FIGHT FOR THE RIGHT.

"The way of the Lord is right!"

Rev. J. CHANDLER.

1. We are fight-ing, dai-ly fight-ing, In the ar-my of the Lord:
2. We are marching, onward march-ing, Toward the fortress of our King:

We've a band of foes to con-quer With the Spi-rit's might-y sword.
Faithful, ac-tive in his ser-vice, Loy-al hearts to him we bring.

While we fight for the right, While we fight for the right, Jesus leads our columns broad;
Hark! the call, "Forward all!" Hark! the call, "Forward all! To the breeze your colors fling!"

While we fight for the right, While we fight for the right, Jesus leads our columns broad.
Hark! the call, "Forward all!" Hark! the call, "Forward all! To the breeze your colors fling;"

3 See our banners proudly floating!
Note our mottoes grand and true!
Will you join us little stranger?
We have work for you to do.—
Chains to break, Souls to take,
Chains to break, Souls to take;
Sin's dark ranks we're marching through.

4 We are fighting, daily fighting;
But our weapons are of love;
All our foes we hope to conquer;
For our help is from above.
Armed in might For the right,
Armed in might For the right,
Steadfast may we ever prove!

IN THE CROSS OF CHRIST I GLORY.

TUNE—AUTUMN.

1 In the cross of Christ I glory,
Tow'ring o'er the wrecks of time:
All the lights of sacred story
Gathers round its head sublime.

2 When the woes of life o'ertake me,
Hopes deceive, and fears annoy,
Never shall the cross forsake me:
Lo! it glows with peace and joy.

3 When the sun of bliss is beaming
Light and love upon my way,
From the cross the radiance streaming,
Adds new luster to the day.

4 Bane and blessing, pain and pleasure,
By the cross are sanctified;
Peace is there, that knows no measure,
Joys that through all time abide.

FADING, STILL FADING.

PORTUGESE. Arranged by W. H. Doane.

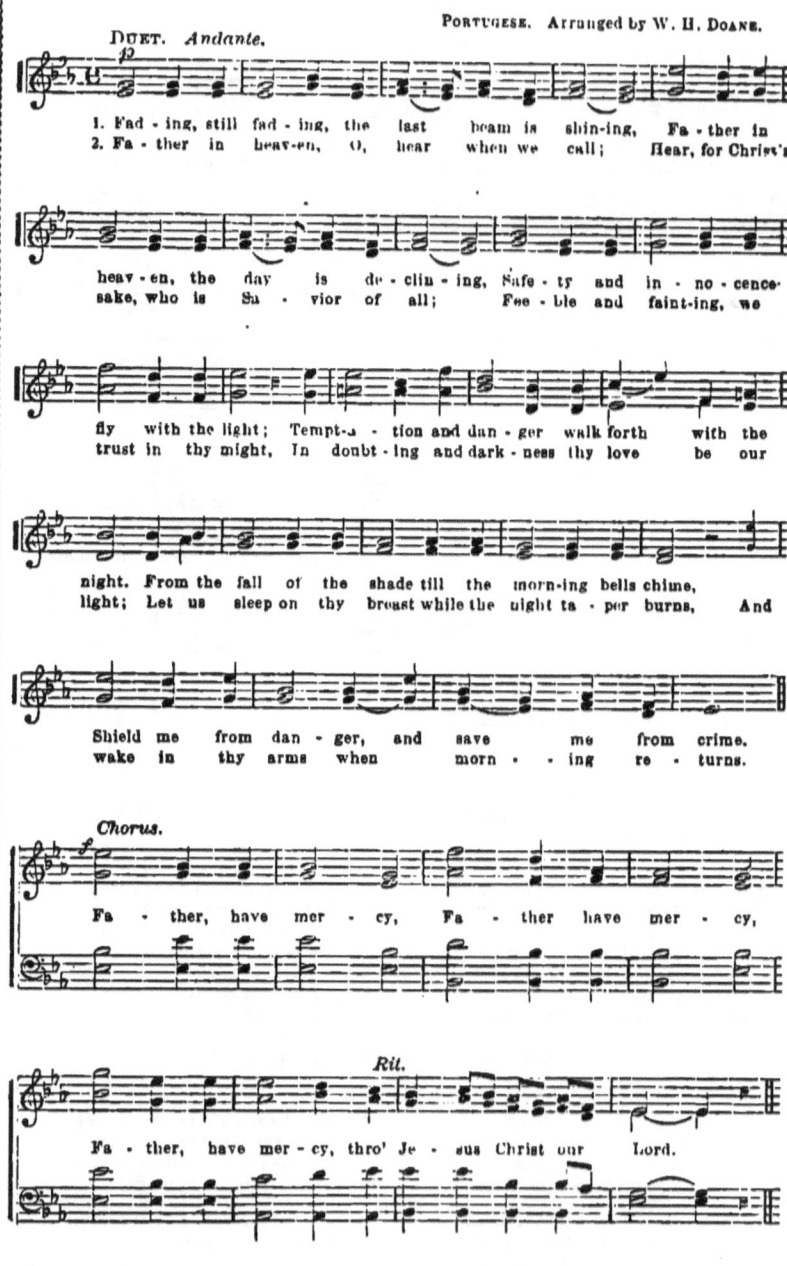

DUET. *Andante.*

1. Fad - ing, still fad - ing, the last beam is shin-ing, Fa - ther in
2. Fa - ther in heav-en, O, hear when we call; Hear, for Christ's

heav - en, the day is de - clin - ing, Safe - ty and in - no - cence-
sake, who is Sa - vior of all; Fee - ble and faint-ing, we

fly with the light; Tempt-a - tion and dan - ger walk forth with the
trust in thy might, In doubt - ing and dark - ness thy love be our

night. From the fall of the shade till the morn-ing bells chime,
light; Let us sleep on thy breast while the night ta - per burns, And

Shield me from dan - ger, and save me from crime.
wake in thy arms when morn - - ing re - turns.

Chorus.

Fa - ther, have mer - cy, Fa - ther have mer - cy,

Rit.

Fa - ther, have mer - cy, thro' Je - sus Christ our Lord.

"COME AGAIN."

From Bradbury's "FRESH LAURELS," by permission.

1. Have you spent a pleas-ant day? Come a-gain, come a-gain, Would you learn the
2. Would you leave all sinful ways? Come a-gain, come a-gain, Would you join our

let-ter way? Then come, come a-gain·   Here you'll find a wel-come true,
cheerful lays. Then come, come a-gain: We are bound for Ca-naan's land,

Hear s that warmly beat for you, They will tell you what to do, O come, come a-
Will ou come and join our band? We will take you by the hand, O come, come a-

gain.   Have you spent a pleas-ant day? Come a-gain, come a-gain;
gain.   Would you leave all sin-ful ways? Come a-gain, come a-gain,

Would you learn the bet-ter way, Then come, come a-gain.
Would you join our cheer-ful lays? Then come, come a-gain.

3 Words of comfort you shall hear,
  Come again, come again,
  From the book we love so dear,
  Then come, come again;
  Jesus suffered on the tree,
  Jesus died for you and me,
  His disciple you may be,
  O come, come again.

4 Come on every Sabbath day,
  Come again, come again,
  Never, never stay away,
  O come, come again;
  Now improve the hours that fly,
  They are gliding swiftly by,
  You are not too young to die!
  Then come, come again.

BLESSED ARE THEY THAT BELIEVE.

Words by FANNY CROSBY.

W. H. DOANE.

1. Come to the fountain of mer-cy and live, Come, and a par-don re-ceive;

Drink of the wa-ter that Je-sus will give, Free-ly to those that be-lieve;

1st.   2d.

Wea-ry and burdened with sorrow, Sweet is the message to thee,
Learn of the meek and the low-ly, Come, heavy la-den, to — me.

Chorus.

Come to the clear flow-ing riv-er, Drink of its wa-ters for-ev-er,

Hungry and thirst-y, O! nev-er, bles-sed are they that be-lieve!

2 Happy the nation whose God is the Lord;
   Hearing in meekness and love
Counsels of wisdom and truth in his word,
   Looking for comfort above;
He is their rock and salvation,
   He is their strength and their song,
Onward from glory to glory,
   Leading them gently along
    Come to the, etc.

3 Look unto Jesus, ye regions of earth,
   Victor of death and the grave,
Tho' he was humble, and lowly his birth
   He is the mighty to save.
Why should we wander in darkness?
   Why to the world should we cling?
Hope, like a bird, is before us,
   Pluming her beautiful wing.
    Come to the etc.

SUNDAY-SCHOOL VOLUNTEER SONG.

From Bradbury's "FRESH LAURELS," by permission.

In marching movement.

1. { We are marching on with shield and ban-ner bright, We will work for God and
   { In the Sunday-school our ar - my we pre-pare, As we ral-ly round our

D. C. We are marching onward, sing-ing as we go, To the promised land where

bat - tle for the right, We will praise his name re - joic-ing in his might, And we'll
bles-sed standard there, And the Sa - vior's cross we ear-ly learn to bear, While we
liv - ing wa - ters flow; Come and join our ranks as pil-grims here be - low, Come and

End.   *Chorus.*

work till Je - sus calls.   Then a - wake,   Then a-

Then   a - wake,

wake,   hap - py song,   hap - py song,   Shout for

Then a - wake,   hap - py song,   hap - py song

D. C.

joy,   Shout for joy,   As we glad-ly march a - long.

Shout for joy,   shout for joy, As we glad-ly march a - long.

2 We are marching on, our Captain ever near;
   Will protect us still, his gentle voice we hear;
   Let the foe advance, we 'll never, never fear,
      For we 'll work till Jesus calls.
   Then awake, awake, our happy, happy song,
   We will shout for joy, and gladly march along;
   In the Lord of hosts let every heart be strong,
      While we work till Jesus calls.

3 We are marching on the straight and narrow way,
   That will lead to life, and everlasting day,
   To the smiling fields that never will decay,
      But we 'll work till Jesus calls.
   We are marching on and pressing toward the prize,
   To a glorious crown beyond the glowing skies,
   To the radiant fields where pleasure never dies,
      And we 'll work till Jesus calls.

HEAVENLY HOME, SWEET HOME.

Words by Miss J. W. Sampson.   Music by W. H. Doane.

1. Heaven - ly home, heaven - ly home, Precious name to me; I

2. Heaven - ly home, heaven - ly home, There no clouds a - rise; No
3. Heaven - ly home, heaven - ly home, Ne'er shall sorrow's gloom, No

love to think the time will come When I shall rest in thee. I've no a - bid-ing cit - y here, I

tear-drops fall, no dark nights dim Thy ever-smiling skies. This earthly home is fair and bright, Yet
doubts nor fears disturb me there, For all is peace at home. I know I ne'er shall worthy be To

seek for one to come; And tho' my pil-grim-age be drear, I know there 's rest at home.

clouds will often come, And O, I long to see the light That gilds my heavenly home.
dwell 'neath heav'n's bright dome; But Christ my Savior died for me, And now he calls me home.

Chorus.   **Repeat Chorus.**

Heavenly home, sweet home, Heavenly home, sweet home, Precious name to me, Home, sweet home.

Heaven - ly home, Heaven - ly home, Precious name to me, Home, sweet home.

Heavenly home, sweet home, Heavenly home, sweet home, Precious name to me, Home, sweet home.

THE DAY IS ENDING.

Contributed to " LITTLE SUNBEAM."　　　　　　　　Rev. R. LOWRY.

1. And now the day is end-ing, With all its toil and care, My
2. For all my sin and fol-ly, This day from morn to even, I
3. While I, my sins con-fess-ing, Implore his pardoning love, I'll

heart to heaven as - cend-ing, Shall of-fer praise and prayer;
pray the Lord most ho - ly That I may be for - given.
praise him for each bles-sing De - scend-ing from a - bove.

The Lord is ev - er mind-ful Of those who seek his face; And
His pleading love most pre-cious I now re-call to mind! The
In - gra-ti-tude is hate-ful; O! keep me from that sin! Lord,

chil - dren, weak and sin - ful, May feel his sav - ing grace.
Lord is ev - er gra-cious, And pit - i - ful and kind.
make me ve - ry grate-ful, And cleanse my soul with - in.

Chorus.

The day of life will soon be end - ing, With its toil and care;

May I, at last to heaven as - cend - ing, Meet my Sa - vior there.

WHERE DO YOU JOURNEY?

Words by MINNIE WATERS.

S. J. VAIL.

Solo.

1. Where do you journey, my bro-ther, O where do you journey, I pray?
2. What is your mission, my bro-ther, What is your mission be-low?
3. O! yes, you will meet us, my bro-ther, God helping our weakness and sin;

Where do you journey, my sis-ter? For stormy and dark is the way.
What is your mission, my sis-ter, As journey-ing onward you go?
Bearing the cross, we, my sis-ter, The crown will endeavor to win.

Duet.

We're journeying onward to Ca-naan, Through suff'ring, and trial, and care,
Our mission is practic-ing mer-cy, Sweet chari-ty, patience and love,
We'll walk through the vale and the shadow, Through suff'ring, and trial, and care,

Ritard.

And when we get safe-ly to glo-ry, O say, shall we meet you all there?
And following the footsteps of Je-sus, That lead to the mansions a-bove,
And when you get safe-ly to glo-ry, You'll meet, yes, you'll meet us all there!

Chorus.

O say, shall we meet you all there? O say, shall we meet you all there?

Ritard.

And when we get safe-ly to glo-ry, O say, shall we meet you all there?

OVER THE RIVER I'M GOING.

MINNIE WATERS.

1 Over the river I'm going,
  Beyond where the pearly gates stand,
Over the cold icy billows,
  To live in a fair, sunny land.
My Father has built me a mansion,
  And filled it with treasures of gold,
Yes, over the river I'm going,
  To where there are pleasures untold.
Chor.—To where there are pleasures untold,
    To where there are pleasures untold;
  Yes, over the river I'm going,
    To where there are pleasures untold.

2 Over the river I'm going;
  O, seek not to draw me aside!
See, for the boatman is waiting
  To ferry me over the tide.
My Savior is there to receive me,
  And shield me from suffering and cold;
Yes, over the river I'm going,
  To where there are pleasures untold.
Chor.—To where there are pleasures untold,
    To where there are pleasures untold'
  Yes, over the river I'm going,
    To where there are pleasures untold.

CLING TO THE BIBLE.

W. H. DOANE.

1. There's a book which surpasses the sages, A vol-ume of wisdom di-vine,
2. 'T is the light which will guide us to glory, The sword of the spirit of might,
3. It reveals where the fountain is flowing, Which washes the soul from its stain,
4. How this book by our fathers was cherished, Their solace, their guide, and
[their rule,

And the glory that gleams from its pages, No splendor of earth can outshine.
And to dwell on its beauti-ful sto-ry, Is of heaven the sweetest delight.
Age and sorrow are comforted knowing, With earth they shall part with their pain.
And our country long since would have perished, But for Bible in church and in
[school.

Chorus.

We'll cling to the Bi - ble, Light of eve-ry land, When

foes shall assail, We'll never, never fail To defend it heart and hand; By the

Bible we will stand, Like a true and valiant army At the Lord's command.

"WAITING, ONLY WAITING."

W. H. DOANE.

1. On - ly wait - ing till the shad-ows Are a lit - tle lon - ger grown,
2. On - ly wait - ing till the reap-ers Have the last sheaf gath-ered home:

On - ly wait - ing till the glim - mer Of the day's last beam is flown,
For the sum-mer time is fa - ded, And the au - tumn winds have come.

☞ Solo for Tenor, or Tenor and Alto, or may be sung as a Quartet.

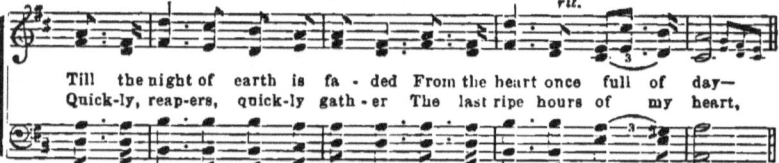

Till the night of earth is fa - ded From the heart once full of day—
Quick-ly, reap-ers, quick-ly gath - er The last ripe hours of my heart,

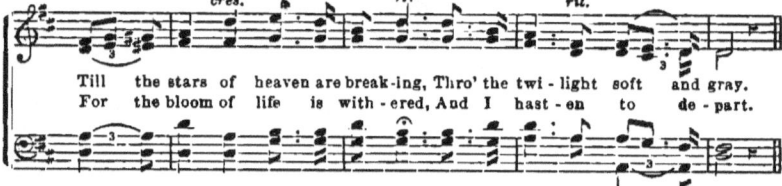

Till the stars of heaven are break-ing, Thro' the twi - light soft and gray.
For the bloom of life is with - ered, And I hast - en to de - part.

Chorus.

Waiting, waiting, waiting till the shadow's
Waiting, waiting, waiting till the shadows are a little longer grown

3 Only waiting till the angels
  Open wide the mystic gate,
At whose feet I long have lingered,
  Weary, poor and desolate.
Even now I hear their footsteps,
  And their voices, far away,
If they call me I am waiting,
  Only waiting to obey.

4 Only waiting till the shadows
  Are a little longer grown,
Only waiting till the glimmer
  Of the day's last beam is done;
Then from out the gathering darkness
  Holy, deathless stars arise,
By whose light my soul shall gladly,
  Tread its pathway to the skies.

"TRIED AND TRUE."

Written for the First Bap. Sab. School, Indianapolis, J. R. OSGOOD, Sup't.

Words by FANNY CROSBY.

W. H. DOANE.

Sprightly.

1. We are a band of mer - ry chil - dren, Full of glee, Full of glee,
2. Hap - py am I the bird is sing - ing, Wild and free, Wild and free,
3. Hap - py am I, the wind is sigh - ing, Tro' the shade, Thro' the shade;

Like the springtime in its beau - ty, Glad are we, Glad are we;
While to the song with hearts we ech - o, So are we, So are we;
Sweet is my home the dai - sy murmurs, In the glade, In the glade;

Bright is the bu - sy world a - round us, Bright with flowers, Bright with flowers,
O! there is joy in ev - ery blossom, We may share, We may share,
Thus we can say in days of childhood, Full of glee, Full of glee,

Smiles from the sun-ny vale a - bove us, Come with the hours, Come with the hor .s.
While we a - dore the hand that made it, Pure and fair, Pure and fair
Blending our hearts with nature's voices, Blest are we, Blest are we

Chorus.

We are a band of mer-ry, mer-ry chil-dren, While to the Sunday-school we cling,

We are a band of mer - ry, mer - ry chil-dren, Tried and true, tried and true.

DON'T YOU HEAR THE ANGELS COMING?

From "HEAVENLY ECHOES," by permission.

DUET. *Soprano and Alto*

1. Ho - ly an - gels, in their flight, Trav-erse o - ver earth and sky,
2. Tho' their forms we can not see, They at - tend and guard our way

Acts of kind-ness their de - light, Winged with mer-cy as they fly.
Till we join their com - pa - ny In the realms of end - less day.

Semi-Chorus of Girls.

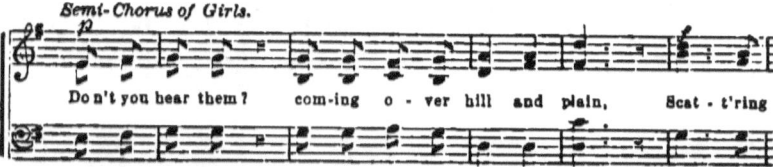

Don't you hear them? com-ing o - ver hill and plain, Scat - t'ring

Chorus.

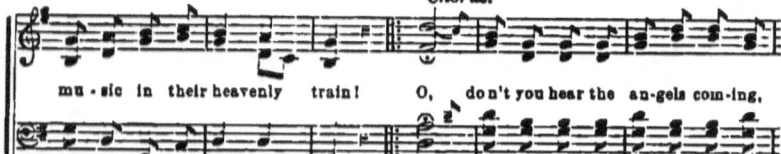

mu - sic in their heavenly train! O, don't you hear the an-gels com-ing,

Sing - ing as they come? O, bear me an - gels, an - gels bear me home!

3 Had we but an angel's wing,
    And an angel's heart of flame,
O, how sweetly would we ring
    Thro' the world the Savior's name.
        Don't you hear, etc.

4 Yet methinks if I should die,
    And become an angel too,
I, perhaps, like them might fly,
    And the Savior's bidding do.
        Don't you hear, etc.

PASS ME NOT.

Words by FANNY CROSBY.

W. H. DOANE.

1. Pass me not, O gen-tle Sa - vior, Hear my hum-ble cry;
2. Let me at a throne of mer - cy, Find a sweet re - lief,

While on oth-ers thou art smil-ing, Do not pass me by.
Kneeling there in deep con-tri-tion, Help my un-be-lief.

Chorus.

Sa - vior, Sa - vior, Hear my hum - ble cry;

While on oth-ers thou art call-ing, Do not pass me by.

3 Trusting only in thy merits
  Would I seek thy face,
  Heal my wounded, broken spirit,
  Save me by thy grace.
    Savior, Savior, etc.

4 Thou the spring of all my comfort,
  More than life to me,
  Whom have I on earth beside thee,
  Whom in heaven but thee?
    Savior, Savior, etc.

COME TO JESUS.

Words by Dr. John B. Peck.

H. P Main.

Tenderly.

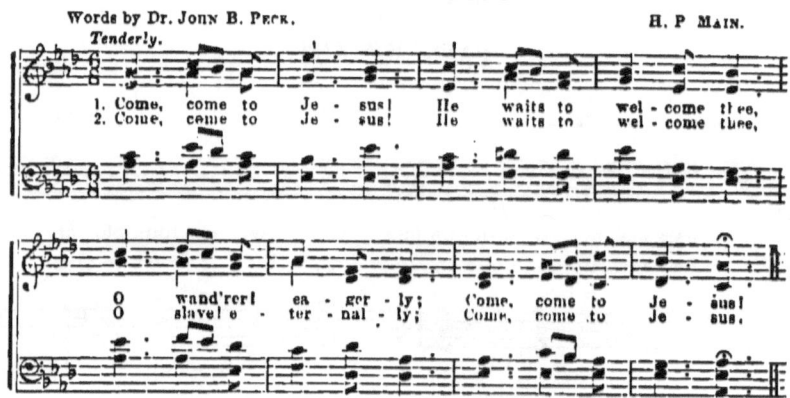

1. Come, come to Je - sus! He waits to wel - come thee,
2. Come, come to Je - sus! He waits to wel - come thee,

O wand'rer! ea - ger - ly; Come, come to Je - sus!
O slave! e - ter - nal - ly; Come, come to Je - sus.

3 Come, come to Jesus!
He waits to lighten thee,
O burdened! graciously;
Come, come to Jesus!

4 Come, come to Jesus!
He waits to give to thee,
O blind! a vision free;
Come, come to Jesus!

5 Come, come to Jesus!
He waits to shelter thee
O weary! blessedly;
Come, come to Jesus!

6 Come, come to Jesus!
He waits to carry thee,
O lamb! so lovingly;
Come, come to Jesus!

I DO BELIEVE. C. M.

1. How sweet the name of Je - sus sounds In a be - liev - er's ear;

Chorus.—I do be - lieve, I now be - lieve, That Je - sus died for me;

D. C.

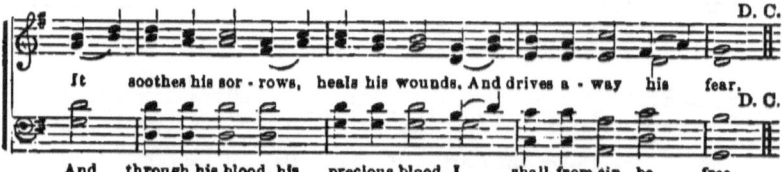

It soothes his sor - rows, heals his wounds, And drives a - way his fear.

D. C.

And through his blood, his precious blood, I shall from sin be free.

2 It makes the wounded spirit whole,
And calm the troubled breast;
'T is manna to the hungry soul,
And to the weary rest.
I do believe, etc.

3 By him my prayers acceptance gain,
Although with sin defiled;
Satan accuses me in vain,
And I am owned a child.
I do believe, etc.

4 Weak is the effort of my heart,
And cold my warmest thought;
But when I see thee as thou art,
I'll praise thee as I ought.
I do believe, etc.

5 Till then I would thy love proclaim
With every fleeting breath;
And may the music of thy name
Refresh my soul in death.
I do believe, etc.

THE FIRE AND CLOUD.

By permission

Henry Tucker.

1. We're marching thro' a wil - der - ness; Marching, marching; We're marching thro' a
2. We're marching thro' a wil - der - ness; Marching, marching; We're marching thro' a

wil - der-ness, Be - set on ev - ery side; We are but a pil - grim band,
wil - der-ness, In search of Ca-naan's land; Soon we'll reach that bliss-ful shore,

Marching toward the promised land, Every foe we can withstand With Jesus for our guide.
Pilgrim days will soon be o'er, Then, in heaven, for evermore, We'll be an an-gel band!

Chorus.

No fears dis-turb us as we go, Nor fill us with dis-may; For

He is a pil-lar of fire each night, A pil-lar of cloud each day.

3 We're marching thro' a wilderness,
   Marching, marching;
We're marching thro' a wilderness,
   Beset on every side;
But the smitten rock will give
Healing draught that we may live;
He will all our sins forgive,
   And every want provide.
      No fears disturb, etc.

4 We're marching thro' a wilderness,
   Marching, marching;
We're marching thro' a wilderness,
   With Christ our beacon-light;
He will lead us thro' the flood,
He will give us daily food;
He will save us by his blood;
   And keep us day and night.
      No fears disturb, etc.

SUNDAY-SCHOOL BATTLE SONG.

From Bradbury's "GOLDEN CENSER," by permission.

THE PORT OF PEACE.

From Bradbury's "FRESH LAURELS," by permission.

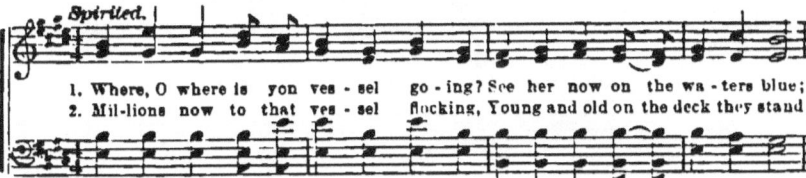

1. Where, O where is yon ves-sel go-ing? See her now on the wa-ters blue;
2. Mil-lions now to that ves-sel flocking, Young and old on the deck they stand,

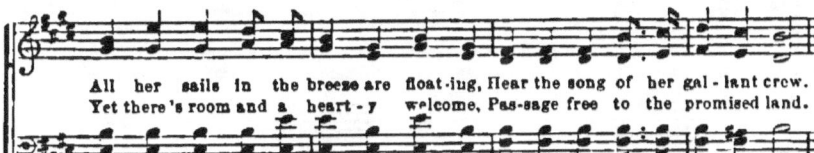

All her sails in the breeze are float-ing, Hear the song of her gal-lant crew.
Yet there's room and a heart-y welcome, Pas-sage free to the promised land.

Chorus.

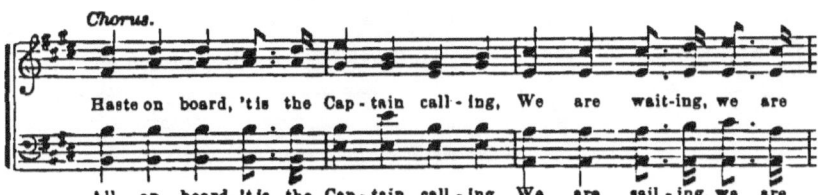

Haste on board, 'tis the Cap-tain call-ing, We are wait-ing, we are
All on board, 'tis the Cap-tain call-ing, We are sail-ing, we are

Chorus to last Stanza.

wait - ing, Pre - cious souls we are bear - ing on - ward,

sail - ing, etc.

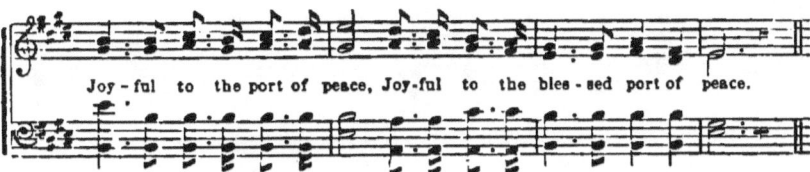

Joy - ful to the port of peace, Joy - ful to the bles - sed port of peace.

3 Praise the Lord, 't is the old ship Zion,
  Jesus is her Captain's name;
  Colors bright from her mast are flying,
  We have heard of her noble fame.
    Haste on board, etc.

4 Quick! on board, she has weighed her anchor,
  Quick! on board, for the wind is fair;
  World, adieu, we are sailing onward,
  Heaven's our home, and our hearts are there.
    Haste on board, etc.

THERE IS JOY FOR YOU.

Words by Mrs. M. A. Kidder.

A. J. Vail.

1. O, let not your hearts be troubled, Nei - ther let them be a - fraid,
2. Let me drink sweet draughts of mercy From the fountain flow-ing free,

For be - hold the bridegroom cometh, In his wed - ding robes ar - rayed.
Let me drink and live for - ev - er, Where my Sa - vior I may see.

Chorus.

There is joy for the ransomed, There is joy for the ransomed, There is
In the peaceful land of Ca-naan, Where the saints sing for - ev - er, Far be-

joy for the ran - somed, There is joy for you.
yond death's rolling riv - er, There is joy for you.

There is joy for you, There is joy for you.

3 Tell me not, ye weary laden,
    There is naught but sorrow here,
For the Lord hath sent his angels,
    And his chosen need not fear.
        There is joy, etc.

4 Keep your lamps well trimmed and burning,
    And the wedding garments nigh,
For no man may know the moment
    Of his coming in the sky.
        There is joy, etc.

THE STORY OF THE CROSS.

"God so loved the world as to give his only begotten Son."

W. H. DOANE.

Soft and Gently.

1. The sto - ry of the cross, To me is ev - er new,
2. They led him to the cross, And there ex - tend - ed high,
3. A - round his hal - lowed tomb The loved dis - ci - ples wept,

I read it o'er and o'er, And tears my cheeks be - dew;
They nailed his hands and feet, While darkness draped the sky;
Three days, with mourn - ful hearts, A lone - ly watch they kept;

In Pi - late's judg-ment hall, I view the Sa - vior now,
He bowed his head and died, The pure and ho - ly one,
But with the Sab - bath morn The dear Re - deem - er rose,

The pur - ple robe, the crown of thorns, That pierced his sa - cred brow.
The tem - ple's vail was rent in twain; The might-y work was done.
The ty - rant death he cap - tive led, And triumphed o'er his foes.

Chorus.

1st. 2d.

O, love unbounded, can it be, He suffered, bled, and died for me?
O, love unbounded, can it be, He lives in heaven and . . pleads for me.

"HAND IN HAND."

Words by FANNY CROSBY.

W. H. DOANE.

1. Now be-gin the heaven-ly race— The Sa-vior calls to-day:
2. He who left his Fa-ther's throne, To suf-fer, bleed, and die,

Let us ear-ly seek his face, And ear-ly learn to pray.
He who made our grief his own, Will ev-ery want sup-ply.

Chorus.

Hand in hand we'll jour-ney on, Reach-ing for-ward to the prize,

Hop-ing, trust-ing in the Lord, Where all our vig-or lies.

3 They who on his name believe,
  And patiently endure,
  Life eternal shall receive,
  And find his mercy sure.
  Hand in hand, etc.

4 Now begin the heavenly race,
  No more, no more delay;
  To the healing fount of grace,
  Rejoicing, haste away.
  Hand in hand, etc.

JESUS, I TURN TO THEE.

"Whoso putteth his trust in the Lord shall be saved."

Words by Mrs. M. A. KIDDER.   W. H. DOANE.

Slow.

1. Je - sus, I turn to thee, Be thou my guide;

Safe in thy lov - ing arms, There let me hide.

No oth - er help I know, No oth - er good be - low,

Noth - ing but earth - ly woe— Noth - ing be - side.

2 Lift up my fainting heart,
 Heavy with sin;
Guilty, and full of wrong,
 Lord, I have been.
Take me, and make me white;
Lord, set my feet aright;
Show me the morning light,
 Savior of men.

3 If thou withhold thy love,
 Where shall I flee?
All will be dark and drear,
 All lost to me.
But if thy Spirit brings
Glory on angel's wings,
My soul hosanna sings,
 Ever to thee.

WEARY OF EARTHLY CARE. 6s & 4s.

1 Weary of earthly care,
 Jesus, my Lord,
I want thy love to share,
 Trust in thy Word.
Come, Savior, from above
Take to thine arms of love,
And from my soul remove
 Each sinful stain.

2 Wash me and make me clean—
 Pure as thou art;
Each root and seed of sin,
 Take from my heart;
Make me, in thought and word,
Like unto thee, my Lord;
Then be thy grace adored
 For evermore.

PURE WITHIN.

Words by FANNY CROSBY.   W. H. DOANE.

1. Lord, on thee my strength re-lies, O, hear me when I call;
2. Rock on which my soul would rest, From storm and tem-pest wild,

Up to thee I lift mine eyes, My life, my help, my all.
Gen-tly pil-lowed on thy breast, Pro-tect thy wea-ry child.

Chorus.

Source of com-fort, spring of grace, Cleanse my heart from ev-er-y sin,

Now re-veal thy smil-ing face, And make me pure with-in.

3 Let thy spirit be my guide,
  To endless joys above;
Grant I may never turn aside,
  Or once forget thy love.
    Source of comfort, etc.

4 Soon my bark will speed its flight,
  To yonder portals fair,
Soon 't will reach the haven bright,
  And drop its anchor there.
    Source of comfort, etc.

KEEP ME, SAVIOR. 7s & 6s.

1 Near me, O my Savior, stand,
  In sore temptation's hour;
Save me with thine outstretched hand,
  And show forth all thy power.
Oh! be mindful of thy word,
  All-sufficient grace bestow:
Keep me, keep me, gracious Lord,
  And never let me go.

2 Never let me leave thy breast,
  From thee, my Savior, stray;
Thou art my support and rest,
  My true and living way,
My exceeding great reward,
  Mine above and mine below;
Keep me, keep me, gracious Lord,
  And never let me go.

"JESUS OF NAZARETH."

Written, by request, for the Anniversary Exercises of the Second Baptist Church, Chicago, January 1, 1869.

W. H. DOANE.

1. What means this eager, anxious throng, Pressing our bus-y streets a-long?
2. Who is this Je-sus? why should he The cit-y move so might-i-ly?

These wondrous gath'rings day by day, What means this strange commotion, say?
A pass-ing stranger, has he skill To move the mul-ti-tude at will?

Duet.

Voi-ces in accents hushed re-ply, Je-sus of Naz-areth passeth by;
A-gain the stirring tones re-ply, Je-sus of Naz-areth passeth by;

rit.

Voices in accents hushed re-ply, Je-sus of Naz-a-reth pass-eth by.
A-gain the stirring tones re-ply, Je-sus of Naz-a-reth pass-eth by.

3 Jesus? 'tis he who once below
Man's pathway trod, 'mid pain and woe;
And burdened hearts where'er he came,
Brought out their sick, and deaf, and lame
Blind men rejoiced to hear that cry,
"Jesus of Nazareth passeth by."

4 Again he comes from place to place,
His holy footprints we can trace:
He pauses at our threshold—nay,
He enters—condescends to stay;
Shall we not gladly raise the cry,
"Jesus of Nazareth passeth by?"

5 Ho! all ye heavy laden, come!
Here's pardon, comfort, rest, and home;
Lost wanderers from a Father's face,
Return! accept his proffered grace.
Ye tempted, there's a refuge nigh,
"Jesus of Nazareth passeth by."

6 But if you still this call refuse,
And do such wondrous love abuse,
Soon will he sadly from you turn,
Your little prayer of pardon spurn:
"Too late, too late," will be the cry,
"Jesus of Nazareth hath passed by."

THE WATCHMAN'S CRY.

W. H. DOANE.

Allegro.

1. Hark! 'tis the watchman's cry, Wake, brethren, wake! Jesus our Lord is nigh,
2. Call to each working band, Watch, brethren, watch! Clear is our Lord's command
2. Heed we the Steward's call, Work, brethren, work! There's work enough for all:

Wake, brethren, wake! Sleep is for sons of night; Children are ye of
Watch, brethren, watch! Be ye as men that wait All at the Master's
Work, brethren, work! This vineyard of the Lord Fresh labor will af-

light; Yours is the glo-ry bright; Wake, brethren, wake!
gate, E'en tho' he tar-ry late, Watch, brethren, watch!
ford; Your is a sure re-ward, Work, brethren, work!

Chorus. pp

Hark! 'tis the watchman's cry, Wake, brethren, wake! Wake, brethren, wake!

Je-sus our Lord is nigh, Wake, breth-ren, wake!

4 Hear we the Shepherd's voice,
Pray, brethren, pray!
Would ye his heart rejoice?
Pray, brethren, pray!
Sin calls for constant fear;
Long as we struggle here,
We need the Strong One near—
Pray, brethren, pray!

5 Now sound the final chord,
Praise, brethren, praise!
Thrice holy is our Lord,
Praise, brethren, praise!
What more befits our tongues,
Leading the angels' songs,
While heaven the note prolongs?
Praise, brethren, praise!

FEED MY LAMBS.

Words by FANNY CROSBY.　　　　　　　　W. H. DOANE.

1. Je - sus stand - ing by the sea, With his faith - ful, cho - sen band,
2. On the young his watch-ful care, Like a shield is kind - ly spread,

Said to Pe - ter, "Lov'st thou me?" When he gave him this command,
Sweet to him the chil-dren's prayer. Sure-ly t was of them he said—

"Feed my lambs," "Feed my lambs," "Feed my lambs."

3 To our Father's throne of grace,
  By our teachers we are led,
  Early taught to seek his face,
  They remember he has said,
  "Feed my lambs."

4 Lambs of Jesus, such are we,
  By his tender mercy led,
  Still our Shepherd he will be,
  He who once to Peter said,
  "Feed my lambs."

WORK FOR GOD.

(Infant Class Song.)

W. H. DOANE.

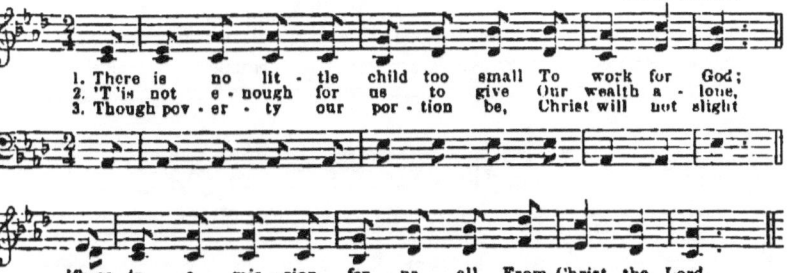

1. There is no lit - tle child too small To work for God;
2. 'Tis not e - nough for us to give Our wealth a - lone,
3. Though pov - er - ty our por - tion be, Christ will not slight

There is a mis - sion for us all From Christ the Lord.
We must en - tire - ly for him live, And be his own.
The low - liest lit - tle one, so be With God be right.

4 The poor, the sorrowful, the old,
  Are round us still;
  God does not always ask our gold,
  But heart and will.

5 Father! O, give us grace to see
  A place for us,
  Where, in thy vineyard, we for thee
  May labor thus.

"WHAT SHALL THE HARVEST BE?"

W. H. DOANE.

Marching time.

1. They are sowing their seed in the daylight fair; They are sow - ing seed in the
2. They are sowing their seed of word and deed, Which the cold know not, nor the

3. Some are sow-ing the seed of no - ble deed, With a sleepless watch and an
4. And there's many yet standing with i - dle hands, Still they're scattering seed throughout
5. Whether sown in the darkness or sown in light; Whether sown in weakness or

noon-day's glare; They are sow - ing seed in the soft twi - light; They are
care - less heed; Of the gen - tle word, and the kind - est deed, That have

earn - est heed; With a cease - less hand in the earth they sow, And the
out the land, And some who are sow - ing the seeds of care, Which their
sown in might; Whether sown in meek - ness or sown in wrath, In the

Chorus.

sow - ing their seed in the sol - emn night. What shall the har - vest be?
blest the sad heart in its sor - est need. Sweet shall the har - vest be;

fields are all whitening where'er they go. Rich will the har - vest be; . . .
soil long has borne, and it still must bear. Sad will the har - vest be; . . .
broad-est highway or the shadowy path. Sure will the har - vest be; . . .

Repeat softly.

What shall the harvest be? - - What shall the harvest be? What shall the harvest be?
Sweet shall the harvest be; - - Sweet shall the harvest be; Sweet shall the harvest be.

Rich will the harvest be; - - Rich will the harvest be; Rich will the harvest be.
Sad will the harvest be; - - Sad will the harvest be; Sad will the harvest be.
Sure will the harvest be; - - Sure will the harvest be; Sure will the harvest be.

"CLIMBING UP ZION'S HILL."

Little ARTIE BAIN, with tremulous voice and moistened eyes, uttered these words
in the class-room.

From "MUSICAL LEAVES."   PHILIP PHILLIPS.

1. "I'm try-ing to climb up Zi-on's hill," For the Sa-vior whispers "Love me;"
2. I know I'm but a lit-tle child, My strength will not pro-tect me;
3. Then come with me, we'll up-ward go, And climb this hill to-geth-er:

Tho' all be-neath is dark as death, Yet the stars are bright a-bove me.
But then I am the Sa-vior's lamb, And he will not neg-lect me.
And as we walk, we'll sweetly talk, And sing as we go thith-er.

Then up-ward still, To Zi-on's hill, To the land of joy and beau-ty,
Then all the time I'll try to climb This ho-ly hill of Zi-on,
Then mount up still God's ho-ly hill, Till we reach the pear-ly por-tals,

My path be-fore Shines more and more, As it nears the gold-en cit-y.
For I am sure The way is pure, And on it comes "no li-on."
Where raptured tongues Proclaim the songs Of the shin-ing-robed im-mor-tals.

Solo, or Semi-chorus.   *Duet, or 2d Semi-Chorus.*

I'm climbing up Zi-on's hill, I'm climbing up Zi-on's hill.

Full Chorus.

Climb-ing, climb-ing, climb-ing up Zi-on's hill.

SAVE ME JESUS.

(Infant Class Song.)

"Those who seek me early shall find me."

Sprightly

W. H. DOANE.

1. Sa - vior thou art ev - er near, Thou my sim - ple prayer wilt hear,

And I plead thy promise kind, "Early seek and ye shall find;" I am vile and

full of sin, Je - sus make me pure with-in, Lead me to the heal-ing flood,

FIRST TIME.   SECOND TIME.

Wash me in thy pre - cious blood, Wash me in thy pre - cious blood.

2 Lord, I want to be thy child,
Make me gentle, meek and mild;
I would pure and holy be,
Teach me how to come to thee.
When I go to work or play,
Be thou with me day by day;
When I seek my little bed,
Let thy wings be o'er me spread

3 Savior, hold me lest I fall,
Deign to hear me when I call,
O, regard my humble cry,
Save me, Jesus, or I die.
Lead me to the healing flood,
Wash me in thy precious blood,
O, regard my humble cry,
Save me Jesus or I die.

WANDERING STRANGER.

W. H. Doane.

First voice.

1. Say, whither wand'ring, stran - ger? Ah! whither dost thou roam, O'er
2. But want and woe have driv - en, The roses from thy cheek; And
3. Come then, benign in - qui. - er, And join me for my way: I'm

this wide world a rang-er, Hast thou no friend or home?
gar - ments rent and riv - en, Thy pov - er - ty be - speak;
journeying to a country, Where beams an end - less day;

Second voice, or answer.

Yes: I've a friend who nev - er Is ab - sent from my
"I've food with which the an - gels Would all de - light - ed
Where saints and an - gels fall - ing Be - fore the great white

side; But I've a home where, ev - er, In peace I shall a - bide.
be! And robes of daz - zling brightness Are now a - waiting me.
throne, To you, to me are call - ing, Haste, pil - grim, hasten home.

Chorus.

Yes, I've a friend who nev - er Is ab - sent from my

side; But I've a home where, ev - er, In peace I shall a-

bide, In peace I shall a - bide.

WAITING FOR THE CROWN.

Words by MRS. M. A. KIDDER.

W. H. DOANE.

DUET.—*Not too fast.*

1 Pressing onward, looking up-ward, To the land of light;
Waiting for a crown of glo - ry Set with jew-els bright

REFRAIN.

Crown of vic-to-ry! crown of beau-ty! We can bear the cross of du-ty, And de-fy the world with its dark frown, Waiting for the crown, Wait-ing for the crown.

2 From the world of peace and beauty,
Angels looking down,
Gladly cheer the earthly pilgrim
Waiting for the crown.
Crown of victory, etc.

3 Thro' the clouds of woe it sparkles
Softly down to earth,
Filling all our hearts with longing
For the heavenly birth.
Crown of victory, etc.

4 Let its bright, celestial glory
All your sorrow drown;
Cheer up, Christian, while you tarry
Waiting for the crown.
Crown of victory, etc.

VERY WEAK.

W. H. Doane.

1. Lord, my heart is ver-y weak, Ver-y weak in-deed,

You who know-est all my thoughts, Knowest all my need.

Chorus.

Sa-vior hear me when I call, Be, O be my all in all;

Sa-vior, hear me when I call, Be my all in all.

2 Be my strength and be my shield,
  Lead me every day;
In the fountain of thy blood
Wash me clean, I pray.
  Savior, hear me, etc.

3 I am nothing in myself—
  May I daily see
All my weakness; while I find
All my strength in thee.
  Savior, hear me, etc.

FLIGHT OF TIME. 7s & 6s.

1 Time is winging us away
  To our eternal home;
Life is but a winter's day,
  A journey to the tomb.
Youth and vigor soon will flee,
  Blooming beauty lose its charm;
All that 's mortal soon will be
  Enclosed in death's cold arm.

2 Time is winging us away
  To our eternal home,
Life is but a winter's day,
  A journey to the tomb.
But the Christian shall enjoy
  Health and beauty soon above,
Far beyond the world's alloy,
  Safe in Jesus' love.

THE OPEN PORTAL.

"And the twelve gates were twelve pearls, and the streets of the city were pure gold."—Rev. xxi: 21.

Words by Rev. Frank M. Ellis.

W. H. Doane.

1. I am sit-ting at the por-tal, With the sap-phire gates a - jar,
2. I am long-ing for that mu - sic, Steal-ing thro' the o - pen door,

Where the eyes of hope im-mor - tal, Catch the gleam-ing world a - far.
And my wea - ry heart grows home-sick, For that land where sin's no more.

Rit.

Chorus.

I'm sit - - ting, I'm sit-ting at the por-tal, I'm
I'm long - - ing, I'm long-ing at the por-tal, I'm

sit - ting, I'm sit - ting, I'm sit - ting at the por - tal.
long - ing, I'm long-ing, I'm long - ing at the por - tal.

3 I am waiting for those loved ones
   Who are with the angel throng,
   To come and bid me welcome;
   But their coming seems so long.
   I'm waiting, I'm waiting,
   I'm waiting at the portal.

4 I am hoping that the Master,
   When my hour has fully come,
   Will give my soul a welcome,
   With the words, "'t is done—well done!"
   I'm hoping, I'm hoping,
   I'm hoping at the portal.

WE'LL GIVE OUR HEARTS TO JESUS.

"Our hearts shall rejoice in him."

Words by FANNY CROSBY.

W. H. DOANE.

We'll give our hearts to Je-sus, And learn his name to praise, The
We'll give our hearts to Je-sus, In sun-ny childhood's hours, When

bles-sed Bi-ble tells us, How pleasant are his ways.
life is like the spring time And full of buds and flowers.

Chorus.

And when we safe-ly an-chor On Ca-naan's hap-py shore,

To him be all the glo-ry, And praise for ev-er-more.

2 We'll give our hearts to Jesus,
    Our best and dearest friend,
  He like a gentle shepherd,
    Will guide us to the end;
  In green and fragrant pastures,
    His little flock will lead,
  Beside the quiet waters,
    Supplying all we need.
      And when, etc

3 We'll give our hearts to Jesus,
    Who died that we might live,
  Our hearts, tho' weak and sinful,
    Are all we have to give.
  The simple prayer of childhood,
    Our God will ne'er despise,
  A lowly contrite spirit,
    Is precious in his eyes.
      And when, etc.

THE MEETING AND THE GREETING.

Words by Mrs. E. H. Gates.   W. H. Doane.

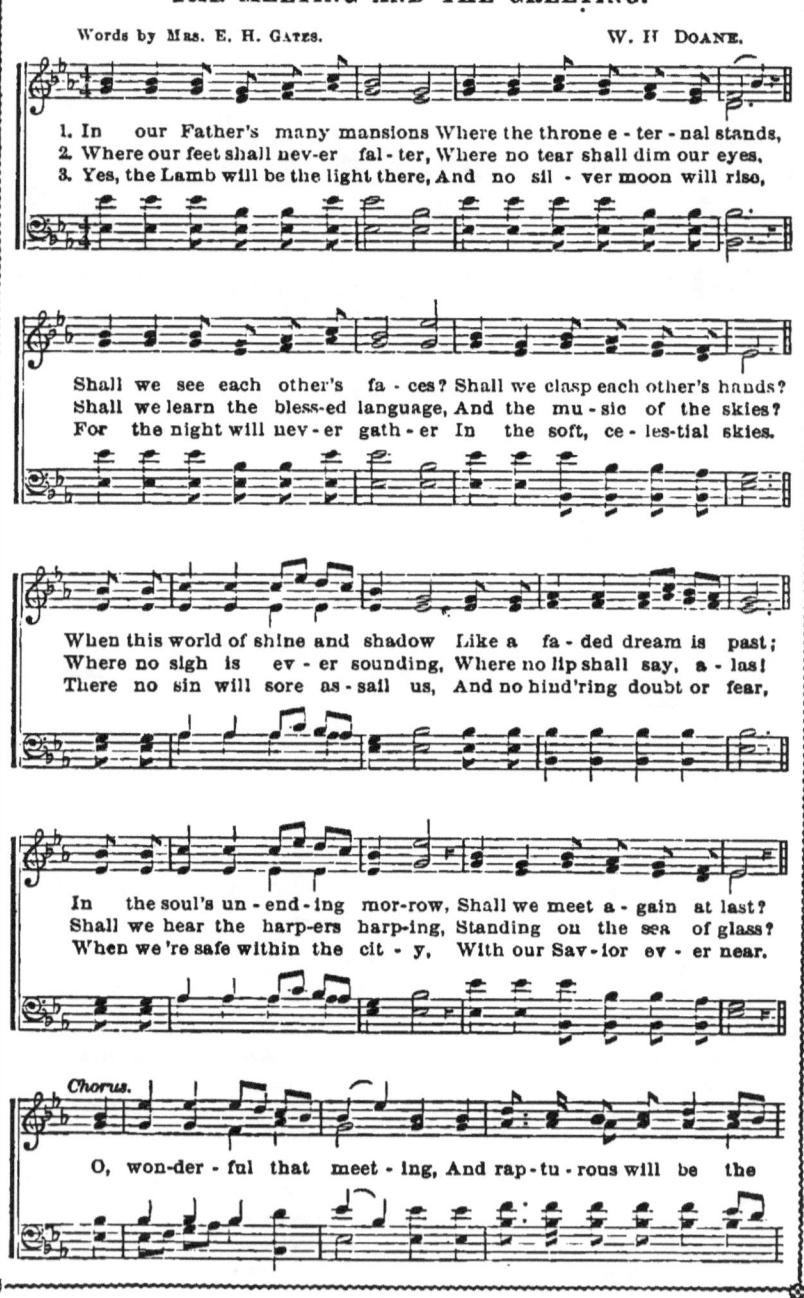

1. In our Father's many mansions Where the throne e - ter - nal stands,
2. Where our feet shall nev-er fal - ter, Where no tear shall dim our eyes,
3. Yes, the Lamb will be the light there, And no sil - ver moon will rise,

Shall we see each other's fa - ces? Shall we clasp each other's hands?
Shall we learn the bless-ed language, And the mu - sic of the skies?
For the night will nev - er gath - er In the soft, ce - les-tial skies.

When this world of shine and shadow Like a fa - ded dream is past;
Where no sigh is ev - er sounding, Where no lip shall say, a - las!
There no sin will sore as - sail us, And no hind'ring doubt or fear,

In the soul's un - end - ing mor-row, Shall we meet a - gain at last?
Shall we hear the harp-ers harp-ing, Standing on the sea of glass?
When we 're safe within the cit - y, With our Sav - ior ev - er near.

Chorus.

O, won-der - ful that meet - ing, And rap-tu - rous will be the

THE MEETING AND THE GREETING. Concluded.

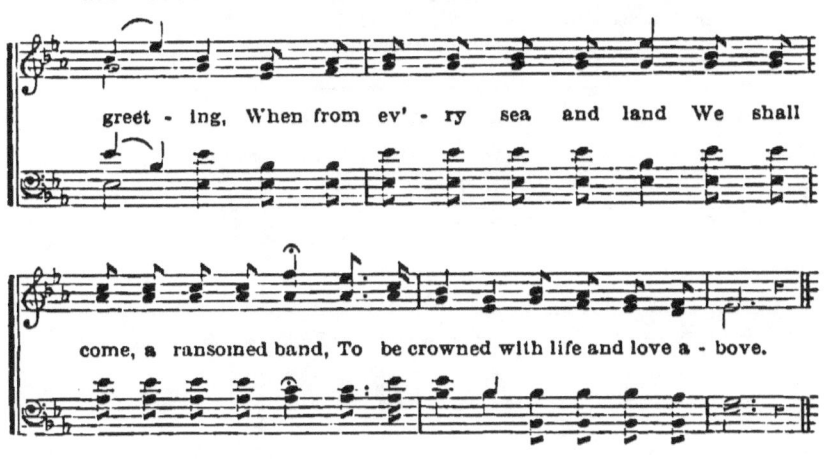

greet - ing, When from ev' - ry sea and land We shall

come, a ransomed band, To be crowned with life and love a - bove.

REST IN JESUS.

Words by Mrs. Van.   W. H. Doane.

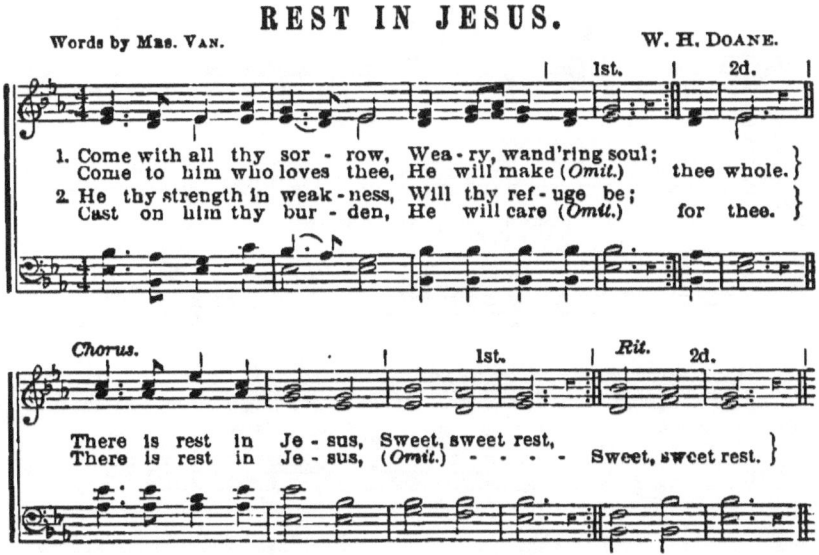

1. Come with all thy sor - row, Wea - ry, wand'ring soul;
Come to him who loves thee, He will make (*Omit.*) thee whole.
2. He thy strength in weak - ness, Will thy ref - uge be;
Cast on him thy bur - den, He will care (*Omit.*) for thee.

Chorus.

There is rest in Je - sus, Sweet, sweet rest,
There is rest in Je - sus, (*Omit.*) - - - - Sweet, sweet rest.

3 Come, in faith believing,
To his will resign;
Ask and he will give thee,
Seek and thou shalt find.
There is rest, etc.

4 See the door of Mercy,
Wouldst thou enter there,
Knock and he will open,
Lo! the key is there.
There is rest, etc.

BEAUTIFUL WITNESS.

I love Jesus, and Jesus loves me; and that is all I've got to say.

Words by FANNIE CROSBY.　　　　　　　　W. H. DOANE.

1. Jimmie, said his kind protector, Long his faithful friend and guide, Jimmie, do you
2. 'T was the Holy Spirit led him In the pleasant way of truth, And he sought and
3. Children, we may love the Savior; If we seek him, we shall find; Are we ready

love the Savior? Yes; the happy child replied. Can you tell how much you love him?
found the Savior In the early days of youth. Should he live till years have sprinkled
now to serve him With our heart, our strength, and mind. Think of all his tender mercies,

All my heart to him I give; Love my Savior? yes, for-ev-er, I will try for
O'er his brow the frost of age, Sweet to him the words of comfort, From the Bible's
All the wonders he has done. Little Jimmie's bright ex-ample Let us fol-low,

Chorus.

him to live. Beau-ti-ful wit-ness for God is he, The
sa-cred page. Beautiful, etc.
ev-ery one. Beautiful, etc.

tears of the or-phan are wiped a-way, I love Je-

sus, and Je-sus loves me; And that is all I've got to say.

"WHO WILL MEET ME?"

"For thou art with me; thy rod and thy staff they comfort me."

By permission.

Geo. F. Root.

1. Who will meet me when I die? Who will lead me to the sky?
2. When my Sa - vior from on high, Calls my spir - it to the sky,

Who will love me in that land? In that spir - it land?
Who will meet me on the strand, Of that spir - it land?

Chorus.

An - gels bright will meet me, An - gels bright, An - gels bright,
An - gels bright, etc.

An - gels bright will meet me, In that spir - it land!

3 Who will hush my trembling heart?
Who will heavenly joy impart?
Who will love me in that land?
In that spirit land?
Angels bright will meet me,
Angels bright, angels bright,
Angels bright will meet me,
In that spirit land!

GIRD ON YOUR ARMOR.

Written for this Work.

W. H. DOANE.

1. Up and a - way, the morn is breaking, Hark! 'tis the Gos - pel
2. Stand by the Cross, like va - liant heroes Wait-ing to hear the
3. Nev - er give up till the foe is vanquished, Nev - er give up till the

Trum - pet's sound; Mar - shal the ranks, the ranks for Je - sus,
Sig - nal Call; Fight for the cause of truth e - ter - nal,
strife is past; Blessed are they who are firm and stead - fast,

Chorus.

Read - y at our post let all be found. Gird on your ar - mor
Fight for the Lord who died for all. Gird on, etc.
They shall be crowned with joy at last. Gird on, etc.

Gird on your ar - mor, Read - y for con - flict in his ar - my;

Un - der his ban - ner, Un - der his banner, Jesus will lead you to victo - ry,

"NO TEARS IN HEAVEN."

For the Death of a Scholar.

Words by FANNY CROSBY.

W. H. DOANE.

Slow and gentle.

1 Our youth is tran-sient as a flower, That blooms, and fades, and dies;
2 The an-gel mes-sen-ger of death, Has gen-tly borne a-way,

Our life is but a sum-mer cloud, And like a shad-ow flies;
A dear com-pan-ion from our side, To realms of end-less day;

Then let us heed the warn-ing voice— To-day its call we hear,
Her voice no more will join with ours The song of praise be-low,

It speaks in deep and sol-emn tones, That come from yon-der bier.
It wakes a pur-er, sweet-er strain, Where on-ly plea-sures flow.

3 When gathered on the Sabbath morn,
    Her vacant place we view,
  We'll think how bright the world she treads,
    And in her steps pursue;
  Be still, let every heart be still,
    And all our sorrow quell,
  We'll bow submissive to his will,
    Who doeth all things well.

THE GATE OF ZION.

W. H. DOANE.

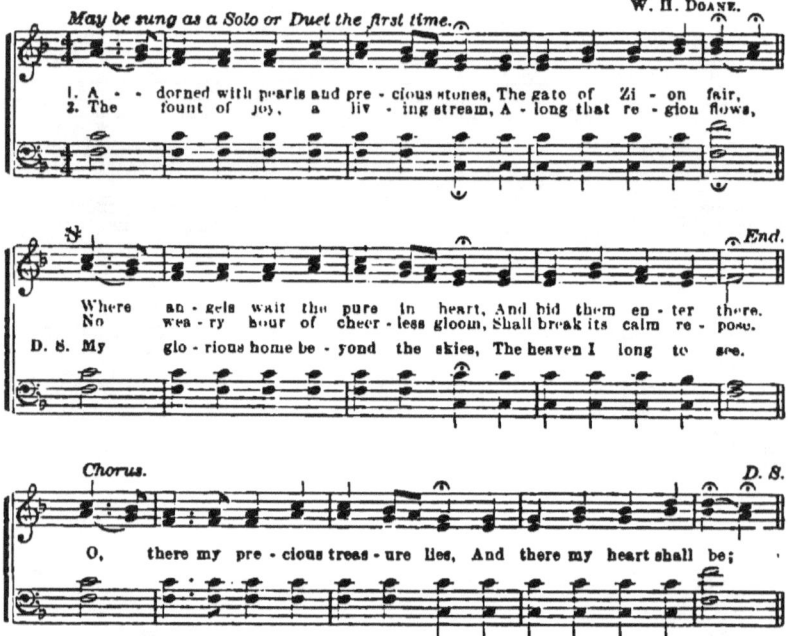

May be sung as a Solo or Duet the first time.

1. A - dorned with pearls and pre - cious stones, The gate of Zi - on fair,
2. The fount of joy, a liv - ing stream, A - long that re - gion flows,

Where an - gels wait the pure in heart, And bid them en - ter there.
No wea - ry hour of cheer - less gloom, Shall break its calm re - pose.

D. S. My glo - rious home be - yond the skies, The heaven I long to see.

Chorus.

O, there my pre - cious treas - ure lies, And there my heart shall be;

3 The Lamb of God, our sovereign Lord,
The shining ones adore,
And kings of earth their glory bring,
To that immortal shore.
O, there, etc.

4 O, let me wing my flight away,
From this vain world of care;
Faith brings me near the gate of pearl—
My soul would enter there.
O there, etc.

GOD IS LOVE.

1 Depth of mercy, can there be
Mercy still reserved for me?
Can my God his wrath forbear,
Me, the chief of sinners, spare?
God is love! I know, I feel;
Jesus weeps and loves me still;
Jesus weeps, he weeps and loves me still.

2 I have long withstood his grace;
Long provoked him to his face;
Would not hearken to his calls;
Grieved him by a thousand falls.
God is love, etc.

3 Now incline me to repent;
Let me now my sins lament;
Now my foul revolt deplore,
Weep, believe, and sin no more.
God is love, etc.

4 There for me the Savior stands?
Shows his wounds and spreads his hands;
God is love! I know, I feel,
Jesus weeps and loves me still.
God is love, etc.

YE VALIANT SOLDIERS.

Key of G.

1 Ye valiant soldiers of the Cross,
Ye happy, praying band,
Though in this world you suffer loss,
You'll reach fair Canaan's land.
Let us never mind the scoffs nor the frowns of
the world,
For we've all got the cross to bear;
It will only make the crown the brighter to
shine,
When we have the crown to wear.

2 All earthly pleasures we'll forsake,
When heaven appears in view,
In Jesus' strength we'll undertake
To fight our passage through.
Let us never, etc.

3 O what a glorious shout there'll be,
When we arrive at home!
Our friends and Jesus we shall see,
And God shall say, "Well done."
Let us never, etc.

OUT OF THE MIRE.

From "Apples of Gold," by permission.

E. Roberts.

1 {The streets of the cit - y are full Of poor, lit - tle, per-ish-ing souls,
{Who wan - der a - way from the light,

2. {Each day there are vic - to - ries won, By thousands and thousands they fall,
{Shall Sa - tan con-tin - ue his war,

In pla - ces that Sa - tan controls! They see not the snare at their feet; They
Un - til he has conquered them all? No! no! with the ar - mor of God, His

know not the dan - ger they're in; Dear Sa-vior! can these be thy lambs, So
darts you may safe - ly de - fy; And O, you must seek for the lambs, Where

Chorus.

changed and disfigured by sin? Famish-ing, per - ish - ing ev - ery day;
Sa - tan has left them to die. Famish-ing, etc.

Lambs of the flock, how they go a-stray! Lambs of the flock, how they go a - stray!

3 Then out of the mire of sin,
   And out of the darkness of night,
Go, bring the dear lambs of the flock,
   And lead them up into the light.
Their voices with tenderness train,
   Their wilfulness strive to subdue,
Be patient and tender with them,
   As Christ has been patient with you.
      Famishing, etc.

4 Beneath all the rags and the dirt,
   That cover a body once fair,
There lieth a jewel of worth,
   More precious than any you wear.
O, let them no longer repine;
   Go find them and tell them their need;
If Jesus' disciple you'd be,
   O, surely his lambs you must feed.
      Famishing, etc.

FLOATING DOWN.

CHAPLAIN McCABE.

Duet.

1. 'Tis said that the ex-ile, who chances to hear, In the land of the stranger, his
2. And thus while he lis-tens to an-thems of praise, Or some soft, stealing melody
3. Nay, he seems to have entered that hea-ven of rest, To have bid-den farewell to tempt-
4. That day of delight, when, an ex-ile no more, His country, his home his loved

own na-tive tongue, Or some 'strain that in child-hood fe-
falls on his ear, Those re-gions of joy he in
a-tion and woes, Al-read-y he joins the bright
friends he re-joins, Tunes his harp to the cho-rus oft

light-ed his ear, Tho' he lis-ten with rap-ture, yet
spir-it sur-veys, And seems the sweet song of the
bands of the blest, Al-read-y par-takes their e-
longed for be-fore, Where sor-row and sigh-ing ne'er

weeps o'er the song, Tho' he lis-ten with rap-ture, yet weeps o'er the song.
ran-somed to hear, And seems the sweet song of the ran-somed to hear.
ter-nal re-pose, Al-read-y par-takes their e-ter-nal re-pose.
blend with the strain, Where sor-row and sigh-ing ne'er blend with the strain.

Chorus.

Floating down, float-ing down, Strains of sweet mu-sic come

Floating down, Float-ing down, Strains, etc.

float-ing down; O, ye ran-somed and glo-ri-fied throng, An

Rit.

ex-ile I wan-der, till I join in your song.

"LEAVE ME WITH JESUS."

Words by Mrs. M. A. Kidder.　　　　　　　　　　　　HENRY TUCKER.

1. Leave me with Je-sus, I ask for no oth-er, Ten-der and pit-i-ful, ev-er the same, He will cling clo-ser to me than a bro-ther, He will bap-tize me a-new in his name.

CHOR.—Leave me with Je-sus, etc.

{ What tho' the clouds and the tem-pests sur-round me, He is my shel-ter, on him I de-pend;
In the deep pit of the tempt-er he found me, Leave me with Je-sus, for he is my friend. }

2 Leave me with Jesus! The surest foundation,
　　Rock for my feet though the floods may o'erflow:
Thro' his dear cross I may hope for salvation,
　　When I have done with my trials below.
What though my father and mother forsake me,
　　What though the friends of my heart disappear,
He, my Redeemer, has promised to take me,
　　Leave me with Jesus, he ever is near.
　　　　Leave me, etc.

3 Leave me with Jesus! When in the dark valley,
　　Helpless and weary I faltering stand,
He his bright angels will speedily rally,
　　White winged seraphs from Canaan's land.
With the dear hand of the Savior to guide me,
　　Bravely I'll enter death's merciless tide,
Safe in his kingdom at last he will hide me,
　　Leave me with Jesus! he too hath died.
　　　　Leave me, etc.

SHALL WE MEET EACH OTHER THERE?

Gently and with feeling.

W. H. DOANE.

1. Shall we meet be-yond the riv - er, Where the sur - ges cease to roll?
2. Shall we meet in that blest har - bor, When our stormy voyage is o'er?

3. Where the mu - sic of the ransomed Rolls in har - mo - ny a - round,
4. Shall we meet with many a loved one, Torn on earth from our embrace?
5. Shall we meet with Christ our Sav - ior, When he comes to claim his own?

Where in all the bright for - ev - er, Sor - row ne'er shall press the soul?
Shall we meet and cast the an - chor By the fair ce - les - tial shore?

And cre - a - tion swells the cho - rus With its sweet, mel - o - dious sound?
Shall we list - en to their voi - ces, And be - hold them face to face?
Shall we hear him bid us wel-come, And sit down up - on his throne?

Chorus.

Shall we meet, shall we meet, Shall we meet each oth - er there?

Shall we meet, shall we meet, Shall we meet each oth - er there?

Repeat, softly.

Shall we meet be-yond the riv - er, Shall we meet each oth - er there?

Shall we meet be-yond the riv - er, Shall we meet each oth - er there?

The Chorus may be repeated if desired.

BROTHERS, WE SHALL MEET AND REST.

Words by JOSEPHINE POLLARD.

W. H. DOANE.

1. When these weary days are o - ver, When our griefs have passed away,
2. Soon the earthly chain will sev - er, Soon to high - er joys we'll rise,
3. Oh, the bliss-ful, joy-ous meeting! Bliss and joy beyond compare!

Like the clouds that melt and van - ish In the sun's ef - ful-gent ray,—
Soon we'll meet the blessed Sav - ior In the realms of Par - a - dise;
When the saints in rap-ture greet - ing, Their Redeemer's love de-clare!

Then, with light, and joy, and glad - ness, Making sunshine in the breast,
Then our hearts will cease to lan - guish, By their load of guilt oppressed;
Storms and doubts shall vex us nev - er, In those mansions of the blest;

Far a - way from sin or sad - ness, Brothers, we shall meet and rest!
There, beyond this toil and an-guish, Brothers, we shall meet and rest!
Safe at home, and safe for - ev - er, Brothers, we shall meet and rest!

Chorus.

Brothers, we shall meet and rest, Meet and rest, yes, meet and rest.

Brothers, we shall meet and rest,

Safe at home, and safe forev - er, Brothers, we shall meet and rest.

ev - er, safe for-ev - er.

124

WE, THE UNDERSIGNED.

"Wine is a mocker, strong drink is raging, and whosoever is deceived thereby is not wise."—PROV. xx: 1.

By permission.   Rev. R. Lowry.

1. We've made up our mind, Don't you see? don't you see? Hearts have been combined,
2. This shall be our song, Ev - ery day, ev - ery day, Shout we loud and long.

We will flee.   Wine-cups ru - by - lined,   Spurn them we, spurn them we;
On our way.   Cups for us shall brim,   Crys - tal bright, dia - mond light!

Chorus.

We, the un - der - signed, Thus a - gree.   We, the un - der - signed,
So shall head and limb   Move a - right.   We, etc.

We, the un - der - signed, We, the un - der - signed, Thus a - gree.

2 Sweet and sparkling flow
Bubbling springs, purling springs;
Pure the grateful glow
Water brings;
Come and pledge us here,
Give the hand, give the hand;
Only water clear
For our band.
We, the undersigned, etc.

4 Scout we dizzy brains,
Tottering walk, reeling walk;
Scout we drunkard's chains,
Mumbling talk;
Water 's our sweet song
Night and day, night and day;
Trill it loud and long,
Yes, for aye.
We, the undersigned, etc.

"CHRIST FOR ME."

W. H. Doane.

1. My heart is fixed, e - ter - nal God, Fixed on thee, fixed on thee;

And my im - mor - tal choice is made, Christ for me, Christ for me!
And while I've breath I mean to sing, Christ for me, Christ for me!

He is my Prophet. Priest, and King, Who did for me sal - va - tion bring,

2 In him I see the Godhead shine,
Christ for me, Christ for me,
He is the majesty divine,
Christ for me, Christ for me;
The Father's well-beloved son,
Co-partner of his royal throne,
Who did for human guilt atone,
Christ for me, Christ for me.

3 To-day as yesterday the same,
Christ for me, Christ for me.
How precious is his balmy name,
Christ for me, Christ for me:
Christ, a mere man, may answer you
Who error's winding way pursue,
But I with past can never do,
Christ for me, Christ for me.

HEAVEN ABOVE. Chant.

W. H. Doane.

1 Sweet home beyond this fading shore, Where pain and sorrow | come no | more
Where all is peace, where all is love, Our blissful home in | heaven a- | bove.

2 On Pisgah's mount in thought we stand, By faith we view our | Fa-ther's | land,
And long to soar on wings of love, Where Jesus reigns in | heaven a- | bove.

3 In peaceful murmurs soft and clear, The pearly stream of | life we | hear,
And catch the mingled strains of love, Where Jesus reigns in | heaven a- | bove.

4 Dear Savior, may thy light divine, In every soul trans- | cend-ent | shine.
Till we shall meet the friends we love, And sing thy praise in | heaven a- | bove.

"COME THOU FOUNT OF EVERY BLESSING."

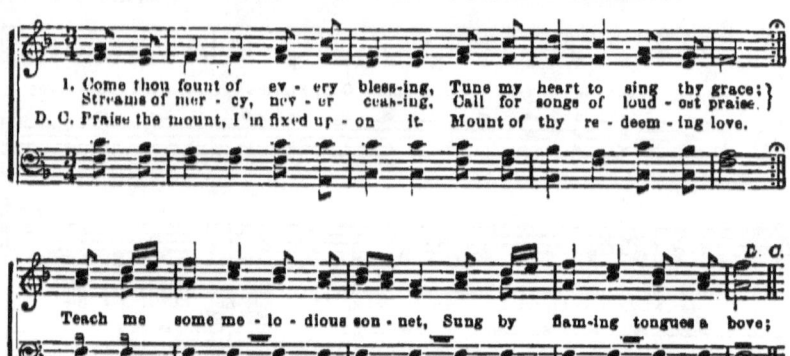

1, Come thou fount of ev - ery bless-ing, Tune my heart to sing thy grace;
Streams of mer - cy, nev - er ceas-ing, Call for songs of loud - est praise.
D. C. Praise the mount, I'm fixed up - on it. Mount of thy re - deem - ing love.

Teach me some me - lo - dious son - net, Sung by flam-ing tongues a bove;

2 Here I raise my Ebenezer,
 Hither by thy help I 'm come,
And I hope, by thy good pleasure,
 Safely to arrive at home.
Jesus sought me when a stranger,
 Wandering from the fold of God,
He, to rescue me from danger,
 Interposed his precious blood.

3 O, to grace how great a debtor,
 Daily I 'm constrained to be!
Let thy goodness, like a fetter,
 Bind my wandering heart to thee.
Prone to wander, Lord, I feel it,
 Prone to leave the God I love,
Here 's my heart, O take and seal it
 Seal it for thy courts above.

ROCK OF AGES, CLEFT FOR ME.

DR. HASTINGS.

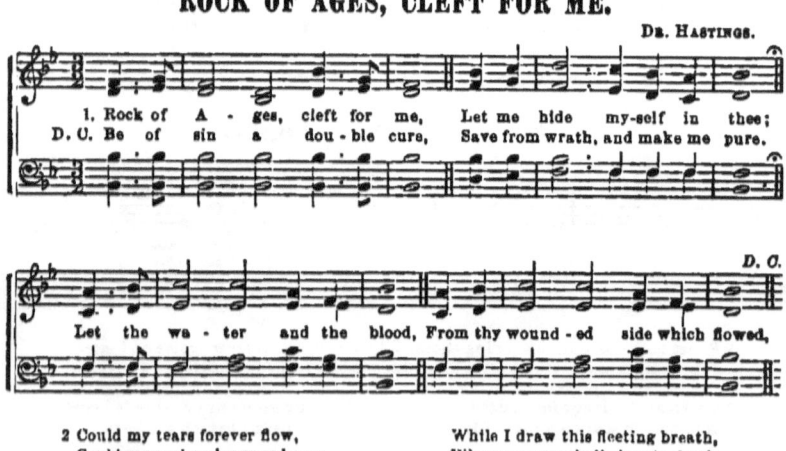

1, Rock of A - ges, cleft for me, Let me hide my-self in thee;
D. C. Be of sin a dou - ble cure, Save from wrath, and make me pure.

Let the wa - ter and the blood, From thy wound - ed side which flowed,

2 Could my tears forever flow,
 Could my zeal no languor know
This for sin could not atone,
 Thou must save, and thou alone;
In my hand no price I bring,
 Simply to thy cross I cling.

While I draw this fleeting breath,
When my eyes shall close in death,
When I rise to worlds unknown,
And behold thee on thy throne,
Rock of Ages, cleft for me,
Let me hide myself in thee.

DENNIS.

NAGELI.

1. Blest be the tie that binds Our hearts in Chris - tian love;
2. Be - fore our Fa - ther's throne, We pour our ar - dent prayers;

The fel - low-ship of kin - dred minds Is like to that a - bove.
Our fears, our hopes our aims are one, Our com - forts and our cares.

3 We share our mutual woes,
Our mutual burdens bear;
And often for each other flows,
The sympathizing tear.

4 When we asunder part,
It gives us inward pain;
But we shall still be joined in heart,
And hope to meet again.

CORONATION. C. M.

HOLDEN.

All Sing.

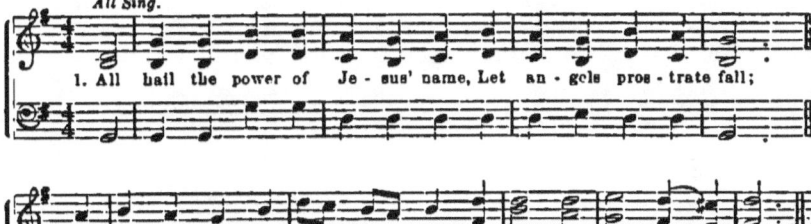

1. All hail the power of Je - sus' name, Let an - gels pros - trate fall;

Bring forth the roy - al di - a - dem, And crown him Lord of all,

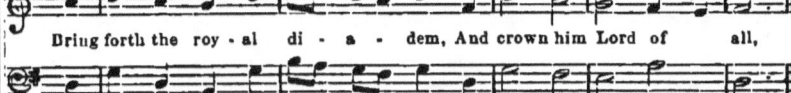

Bring forth the roy - al di - a - dem, And crown him Lord of all.

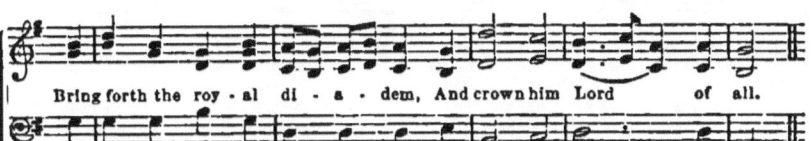

2 You chosen seed of Israel's race,
A remnant weak and small,
Hail him who saves you by his grace,
And crown him Lord of all.

3 You Gentile sinners, ne'er forget
The wormwood and the gall;
Go, spread your trophies at his feet,
And crown him Lord of all.

4 Let every kindred, every tribe,
On this terrestrial ball,
To him all majesty ascribe,
And crown him Lord of all.

5 O, that with yonder sacred throng,
We at his feet may fall!
We 'll join the everlasting song,
And crown him Lord of all.

O, HOW I LOVE JESUS!

" We love him, because he first loved us "—JOHN iv: 19.

Arr. by W. H. DOANE.

1. A - las! and did my Sa - vior bleed? And did my sov' - reign die?
2. Was it for crimes that I had done He groaned up - on the tree?

Would he de - vote that sa - cred head For such a worm as I?
A - maz - ing pit - y! grace un-known! And love be - yond de - gree!

Chorus.

O, how I love Je - sus, O, how I love Je - sus,

O, how I love Je - sus, Be - cause he first loved me.

3 Well might the sun in darkness hide,
  And shut his glories in,
When God's own Son was crucified
  For man the creature's sin.
    O, how I, etc.

4 Thus might I hide my blushing face
  While his dear cross appears,
Dissolve my heart in thankfulness,
  And melt mine eyes to tears.
    O, how I, etc

5 But drops of grief can ne'or repay
  The debt of love I owe;
Here, Lord, I give myself away;
  'T is all that I can do.
    O, how ↓, etc.

WATCH AND PRAY.

By permission.

Rev. R. Lowry.

1. Watch, for the time is short; Watch, while 't is called to - day;
2. Chase slum - ber from thine eyes; Chase doubt - ing from thy breast
3. Take Je - sus for thy trust: Watch, watch, for ev - er - more;

Watch, lest the world pre - vail; Watch, Chris-tian, watch and pray;
Thine is the prom - ised prize Of heaven's e - ter - nal rest;
Watch, for thou soon must sleep With thou-sands gone be - fore.

Watch, for the flesh is weak; Watch, for the foe is strong;
Watch, Chris-tian, watch and pray; Thy Sa - vior watched for thee,
Now, when thy sun is up, Now, while 't is called to - day,

Watch, lest the bride-groom come; Watch, though he tar - ry long.
Till from his brow they poured Great drops of ag - o - ny.
Now is ac - cept - ed time; Watch, Chris-tian, watch and pray.

Chorus

O, watch and pray; O, watch and pray;

O, watch and pray; O, watch and pray; O, watch and pray; O, watch and pray; O,

watch in the dark - ness, and watch in the day; Chris - tian, watch and pray.

THERE'LL BE REST BY AND BY.

Words by JOSEPHINE POLLARD.

W. H. DOANE.

Duet.

1. We must toil in the heat of the day, From the dawn until daylight appears; For swift-ly are pass-ing a-way
2. We must work for the promised reward, We must strive for the crown we're to wear, And when-ev-er we're called by our Lord,

swift-ly are pass-ing a-way To the land where we'll la-bor no more.
ev-er we're called by our Lord, We must work for him faith-ful-ly there.

Chorus.

There'll be rest, by and by; There'll be rest, by and by, by and by;

There'll be rest, by and by, by and by;

There'll be rest, by and by; There'll be rest, by and by, by and by.

There'll be rest, by and by, by and by.

3 We are weak, but the Savior is strong,
And his grace he will freely supply;
Though the time of our trial seem long,
Yet we know we shall rest by and by.
There'll be rest, etc.

4 In the land where our sighing will cease,
Where no sorrow shall ever come nigh;
In that land of contentment and peace
We shall rest, we shall rest by and by.
There'll be rest, etc.

THE ANGEL BOATMAN.

Words by Mrs. Lydia Baxter.

T. E. Perkins.

1. One by one we cross the riv - er, One by one are fer - ried o'er;
2. One by one we come to Je - sus, As we heed his gen - tle voice;

One by one the crowns are giv - en On the bright, ce - les - tial shore,
One by one his vine-yard en - ter, There to la - bor and re - joice.

Youth and childhood oft are pass - ing O'er the dark and roll - ing tide, - -
One by one sweet flow'rs we gath - er In the glorious work of love, - -

And the white-robed an - gel boat - man Is the dy - ing Christian's guide;
Gar - lands for the an - gel boat - man To con - vey to realms a - bove;

And the white-robed an - gel boat - man Bears them o'er the roll - ing tide.
And the white-robed an - gel boat - man Bears them to the realms of love.

3 One by one the heavy-laden
    Sink beneath the noontide sun;
And the aged pilgrim welcomes
    Evening shadows as they come.
One by one, with sins forgiven,
    May we stand upon the shore,
Waiting till the angel boatman
    Takes the helm, and guides us o'er;
And the white-robed angel boatman
    Lands us on the shining shore.

THE JASPER SEA.

Words by J. P.

W. H. DOANE.

1. When we've crossed the Jas - per sea, To the oth - er shore;
2. With the an - gels round the throne, Robed in white we'll stand;

Full of bliss our songs shall be, Prais - ing ev - er - more.
Death and tears are nev - er known In that hap - py land.

Chorus.

When we reach the shore, O'er the Jas - per sea; Joy shall reign for

When we reach the shore,

Rit.

ev - er-more, And heaven our home will be, And heaven our home will be.

3 Captive chains shall bind no more,
When death sets us free;
When we reach the other shore,
O'er the Jasper sea.
When we reach, etc.

4 Parting days will never come;
Bright our lot will be;
When we reach our heavenly home
O'er the Jasper sea.
When we reach, etc.

5 To the judgment-seat above,
Swiftly we repair;
Saved from wrath through Jesus' love,
We shall see him there,
When we reach, etc.

EVER GUIDE ME.

Words by J. P.

W. H. DOANE.

1. Ev - er guide me, gen - tle Sav - ior, Through the drear - y paths of sin,
2. Earthly scenes may tempt me sore - ly, Earth - ly cares op - press my soul;

D C. Ev - er guide me, etc.

End.

In the ear - ly days of child - hood, Let my trust in thee be - gin.
Be thou near me, gen - tle Sav - ior, By thy grace my fears con - trol.

Chorus.

Ev - er guide me, gen - tle Sav - ior, Keep me in the straight and narrow way;

D. C.

From thy lov - ing smile and fa - vor Nev - er, nev - er let me stray.

3 When from thee my footsteps wander,
When my heart grows dull and cold,
Lead me, gentle Shepherd, lead me
Unto thy dear flock and fold.
Ever guide me, etc.

"LOOK TO JESUS."

Words by JOSEPHINE POLLARD.

W. H DOANE.

1. Look to Je-sus, wea-ry one, Full of an-guish, full of grief; He will com-fort; he a-lone Has the balm for thy re-lief. *Rit.* Look to him in thy de-spair, Rest and refuge he will give; All thy burdens he will

"LOOK TO JESUS." Concluded.

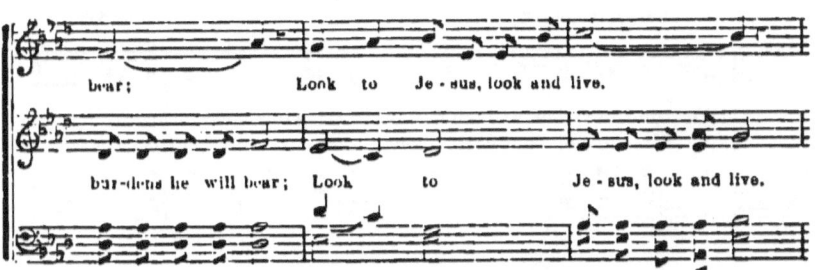

2 See, the loving Savior stands,
  Pleading for thy fond embrace;
Trust thyself to Jesus' hands,
  In his bosom hide thy face;
All thy sickness he can cure,
  All thy sins he will forgive,
He will make his promise sure;
  Look to Jesus, look and live.

3 Look to Jesus; not in vain
  Shall the weary seek for rest;
Weep away thy tears and pain,
  Like a child, upon his breast.
Breathe thy sorrows in his ear;
  Strength for every day receive,
Light in darkness will appear,
  If thou wilt but look and live.

SHINING SHORE.

1 My days are gliding swiftly by,
  And I, a pilgrim stranger,
Would not detain them as they fly,
  Those hours of toil and danger.

Chorus. For now we stand on Jordan's strand,
  Our friends are passing over;
And just before the shining shore
  We may almost discover.

2 We'll gird our loins, my brethren dear,
  Our heavenly home discerning;

Our absent Lord has left us word,
  Let every lamp be burning.

3 Should coming days be cold and dark,
  We need not cease our singing;
That perfect rest naught can molest
  Where golden harps are ringing.

4 Let sorrow's rudest tempest blow,
  Each cord on earth to sever,
Our King says come, and there's our home,
  Forever? O, forever!

136

WE COME TO-DAY.

Words by Josephine Pollard.　　　　　　　　　　W. H. Doane.

1. We come, we come without de-lay, To sing our songs of love to-day,
2. We come to blend our voices sweet, In songs of praise at Je-sus' feet;

Our joyous hearts in praise arise, And ech-oes fill the a-zure skies.
He is our life—to him we owe Whate'er of bliss we meet be-low.

Chorus.

We come, we come, 'Tis love hath led us all the way;
We come, we come, We

We come, we come, We come, we come to-day.
come, We come,

3 To him we look for daily bread,
By whom alone we're daily fed;
In all our griefs he has a share,
And he alone can answer prayer.
We come, etc.

4 We come, we come without delay
To Jesus' feet we come to-day;
'Tis there we lay our burdens down,
And there the cross becomes our crown.
We come, etc.

ONLY LOOK TO JESUS.

"Look unto Me, and be ye saved."—Isa. xlv: 22.

Words by T. McDougall.   W. H. Doane.

1 Look un-to Me, ye wea-ry ones, With wounded spirits grieving;
2. When weary with your load of sin, Your heart is sad and lone-ly,
3. When sorrow like a troubled sea, Rolls o'er your weary spir-it;

Here par-don free for-ev-er flows To all who look be-liev-ing.
O! turn a-way from all with-in, And look to Je-sus on-ly.
In-sweetest tones He calls to thee, Look un-to Me and bear it.

Chorus.

On-ly look a-way to Him, On-ly turn a-way from sin, To the

bleeding Lamb who died to save us; On-ly look a-way to Him, He will

soft-ly en-ter in To the wea-ry heart that longs for Je-sus.

STRIKE FOR JESUS.

Written, by request, for the Bethel Mission Sabbath-School, Hartford, Conn.,
E. J. Canfield, Superinteudent.

W. H. DOANE.

Not too fast.

1. Strike! strike for Jesus, Soldiers of the Lord! Hoping in his mercy,
2. What though raging lions Meet us on the way, Zionward we're marching
3. Strike! strike for Jesus He - roes of the cross Sac - ri - fi - cing pleasure,
4. Hand to hand u - ni - ted, Heart to heart as one, Let us still keep marching

Trust - ing in his word. Lift the Gospel ban - ner High above the world,
T'ward the gates of day. An - gel Spirits guiding, Point us to the light,
Glo - ry - ing in loss. Bind the helmet stronger, Tighter grasp the sword,
Till our journey 's done. Till we see the an - gels Come in glo - ry down,

Chorus. Allegro.

Let its folds of beau-ty Ev - er be un-furled. Strike! strike for Jesus,
Com - ing o-ver Jordan, From our home in sight. Strike, etc.
Conquering and to conquer, Bat-tle for the Lord. Strike, etc.
With the shining garments, And the victor's crown. Strike, etc.

He - roes be, Fight till the vic-tory You shall see; Strike! strike for

Je - sus, Ne'er give o'er, Rest, then, in glo - ry, Ev - er - more.

ANGELS ARE CALLING ME.

W. H. DOANE.

1. I feel in my soul the as-sur-ance of faith That
2. Then why should I mourn, tho' the star of my life May
3. I hear them in sor-row, I hear them in joy, They

Je-sus my por-tion will be; I know in the man-sion that
wane in the sky where it shone; Tho' all that en-cir-cle my
come in the si-lence of night, And waft the sweet fragrance of

he has pre-pared, The an-gels are wait-ing for me.
path-way be-low, Should perish and leave me a-lone?
ros-es that bloom, In E-den's fair land of de-light.

Chorus.

An-gels, bright an-gels are call-ing me, call-ing me, call-ing me,

An-gels, bright angels are call-ing me Home to the beau-ti-ful land.

4 I know they will come when my journey is o'er,
And bear me across the dark sea;
But dearer, far dearer, more precious than all,
My welcome from Jesus will be.

WORK FOR JESUS.

Words by Thos. McDougall.

W. H. Doane.

1. Oh, come and work for Je - sus, With cheerful hearts and true,
2. Come, let us work for Je - sus, By faith and earnest prayer,
3. Come, let us work for Je - sus, We've ma - ny jew - els rare

And tell the love of Je - sus, Who bled and died for you;
The lit - tle ones in Je - sus should claim our constant care;
To gath - er yet for Je - sus, Who will their lus - tre wear;

Oh, come and work for Je - sus, In sunshine or in rain,
Come, let us work for Je - sus, For hearts are bleeding sore,
Then let us work for Je - sus Be - fore the sun goes down,

The seed you sow for Je - sus Shall not be sown in vain.
While 'neath the wings of Je - sus There's healing ev - er - more.
We've hearts to win for Je - sus Ere we can wear a crown.

Chorus.

Then work, gladly work for Je - sus, There's a glorious work for all; Work a-

way with the day, Till the shadows fall, Then go home and wear a crown.

BY THE CRYSTAL RIVER.

Words by Dr. C. R. Blackall.

W. H. Doane.

1. Gathered by the Crys-tal Riv-er, Toil and bur-den whol-ly past,
2. Waiting by the Crys-tal Riv-er, For the loved ones yet to come,
3. Rest-ing by the Crys-tal Riv-er, Filled with Jesus' love and light,
4. Chanting by the Crys-tal Riv-er, Songs redeemed a-lone can sing,

Life's dark ma-zes gone for-ev-er, We shall gain our home at last.
We shall meet where naught can sever, Welcome to their promised home.
Dwell-ing in his presence ev-er, We shall know no clouds or night.
We shall live and reign for-ev-er, One in Christ our ris-en King.

Chorus.

O! pure flowing stream from Golden Throne! O! sweet song of host that

Christ has won! Joy-ous an-thems to our King, Through the

arch-es broad shall ring, Hal-le-lu-jahs to Him who rules a-lone.

COME, SINNER, TO JESUS.

Words by Mrs. E. M. H. Gates.

W. H. Doane.

1. Come, sinner, to Jesus, O, hear him entreating, Come follow his voice :t will
2. Come, sinner, to Jesus, Your cares and your crosses Lay down at his feet, an..i?
3. The battle! the battle! how sorely it rages, Our foes are without, and our
4 He will hide you from harm in his secret pavilions, His angels will guard you by

lead to the skies; Commit now thy heart and thy life to his keeping, That the
tenderness prove; Bring hither your doubts and your fears and your losses, And
foes are within; The strife has been long, it has lasted for a-ges, The
night and by day; You shall join in the song of the witnessing millions, Who

Chorus.

light of his love on thy darkness may rise. Behold, he comes quickly! O,
rest in his promi - ses, rest in his love. Behold, etc.
bat - tle with sorrow, the bat - tle with sin. Behold, etc.
washed, in his blood, their transgressions away. Behold, etc.

haste to adore him, March under his banner, and joyfully sing; The crowns of the

world shall be cast down before him, This mighty, eternal, all-conquering King!

OUR SONG OF TRIUMPH.

By permission.

Words and Music by Rev. ALFRED TAYLOR.

1. March a - long! march a - long! Sing-ing a glad, tri - umphant song.
2. March a - long! march a - long! Sing-ing a glad, tri - umphant song.
3. March a - long! march a - long! Sing-ing a glad, tri - umphant song.
4. March a - long! march a - long! Sing-ing a glad, tri - umphant song.

Semi-Chorus.

Sing of the love of God to me, Sing of his grace so rich and free;
Sing what he tells me in his word, Brightest and best that e'er was heard;
Sing how he loved my soul so well, Ransomed with blood from sin and hell;
Sing of my Je-sus, strong to save, Sing of his vic-tory o'er the grave;

Chorus.

Sing of his goodness by the way, Sing how he keeps me day by day.
Sing how my Savior came to die, Sing how he lives and reigns on high.
Sing how his precious blood was spilt, Washing a-way my deep-est guilt.
Sing how he rose from death and night, Bringing my soul to end-less light.

Duett.

Sing of the mer-cy, sing of the love, Keeping my soul for glo-ry a-bove;

March a - long! march a - long! Sing-ing a glad, tri-umph-ant song.

FATHER, HEAR OUR PRAYER.

(Hymn Chant.)

W. H. DOANE.

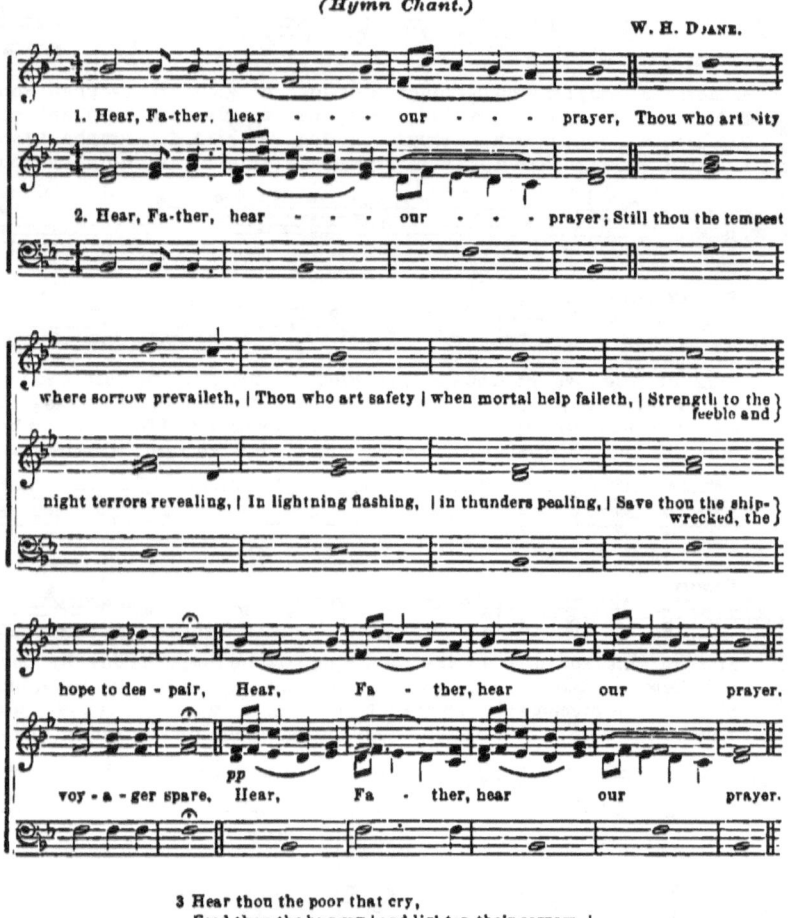

1. Hear, Fa-ther, hear our prayer, Thou who art
where sorrow prevaileth, | Thou who art safety | when mortal help faileth, | Strength to the feeble and hope to des - pair, Hear, Fa - ther, hear our prayer.

2. Hear, Fa-ther, hear our prayer; Still thou the tempest
night terrors revealing, | In lightning flashing, | in thunders pealing, | Save thou the ship-wrecked, the voy - a - ger spare. Hear, Fa - ther, hear our prayer.

3 Hear thou the poor that cry,
Feed thou the hungry | and lighten their sorrow, |
Grant them the sunshine | of hope for the morrow, |
They are thy children, their | trust is on high—
Hear thou the poor that cry

4 Dry thou the mourner's tear,
Heal thou the wounds | of time-hallowed affection, ,
Grant to the widow | and orphan protection, |
Be, in their trouble, | a friend ever near,
Dry thou the mourner's tear.

5 Hear, Father, hear our prayer;
Long hath thy goodness | our feet attended, |
Be with the pilgrim | whose journey is ended. |
When at thy summons for | death we prepare,
Hear, Father, hear our prayer?

EVENING HYMN. 7s.

QUARTETTE.

BREMER.

Andante.

1. Sav - ior breathe an even - ing blessing, Ere repose our spir - - its seal;
2. Though destruction walk a - round us, Though the arrows past us fly,

3. Though the night be dark and dreary, Darkness can not hide from thee;
4. Should swift death this night o'er-take us, And our couch be-come our tomb,

Sin and want we come con - fessing, Thou canst save, and thou canst heal.
An - gel - guards from thee surround us, We are safe if thou art nigh.

Thou art he who, nev - er weary, Watcheth where thy people be.
May the morn in heaven a - wake us, Clad in bright and deathless bloom.

THE GUIDING HAND. Hymn Chant.

S. J. VAIL.

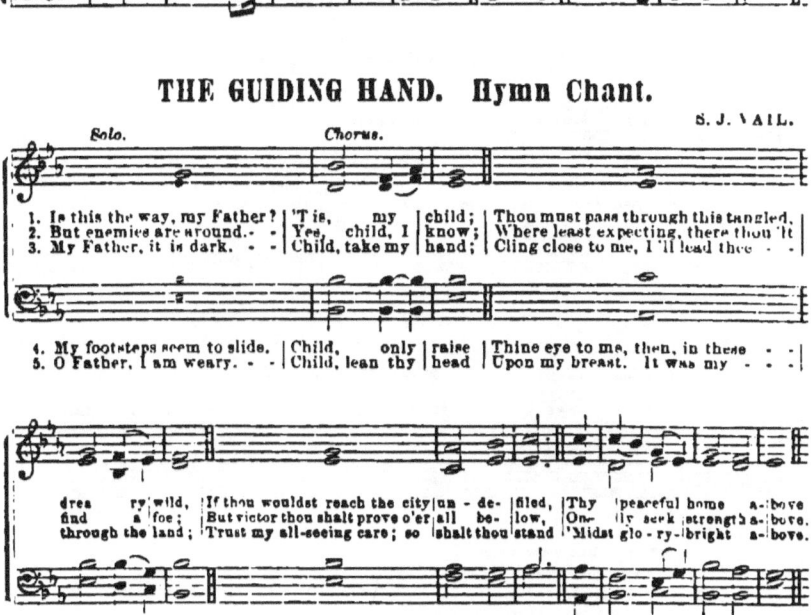

Solo.   *Chorus.*

1. Is this the way, my Father? |'T is, my | child; | Thou must pass through this tangled,
2. But enemies are around.- | Yes, child, I | know; | Where least expecting, there thou 'lt
3. My Father, it is dark. - - | Child, take my | hand; | Cling close to me, I 'll lead thee - -

4. My footsteps seem to slide. | Child, only | raise | Thine eye to me, then, in these - -
5. O Father, I am weary. - - | Child, lean thy | head | Upon my breast. It was my - - -

drea ry|wild, |If thou wouldst reach the city|un - de-|filed, |Thy |peaceful home a-|bove
find a |foe; |But victor thou shalt prove o'er|all be-|low, |On- |ly seek strength a-|bove.
through the land; |Trust my all-seeing care; so |shalt thou |stand |'Midst glo-ry-|bright a-|bove.

slip - pery |ways; |I will hold up thy goings;- |-|thou shalt|praise |Me |for each |step, a-|bove.
love that |spread Thy rugged path; hope on till| I |have|said, |Rest, |rest, for |aye, a-|bove.

THE WAY IS DARK.

(Chant.)

W. H. DOANE.

1. O! Father, hear! The way is dark, and I would } fain discern What steps to take, into which } path to turn;
2. My faith is weak! I long to hear thee say, "This } is the way; Walk in it, fainting soul, I 'll } be thy stay;"

3. Let thy strong arm } Reach through the gloom for me to } lean upon, And with a willing heart I 'll } journey on,
4. I wait for thee As those who, watching, wait the } coming dawn, Pant, as for water pants the } thirsty fawn;

Ritard.

O! make it clear,   O! make it clear,   O! make it clear.
Speak, Savior, speak!   Speak, Savior, speak!   Speak, Sa - vior, speak!

And fear no harm,   And fear no harm,   And fear no harm.
O! come to me,   O! come to me,   O! come to me.

MAKE ME THANKFUL.

W. H. DOANE.

1. Je - sus, ten - der Sa - vior, Hast thou died for me?
2. When the sad, sad sto - ry Of thy grief I read,

Make me ve - ry thank - ful In my heart to thee
Make me ve - ry sor - ry For my sins, in - deed

3 Now, I know thou lovest,
And dost plead for me;
Make me very thankful
In my prayers to thee.

4 Soon, I hope, in glory,
At thy side to stand;
Make me fit to meet thee
In that happy land.

TELL IT TO JESUS.

Hymn Chant.

Words by FANNY CROSBY. W. H. DOANE.

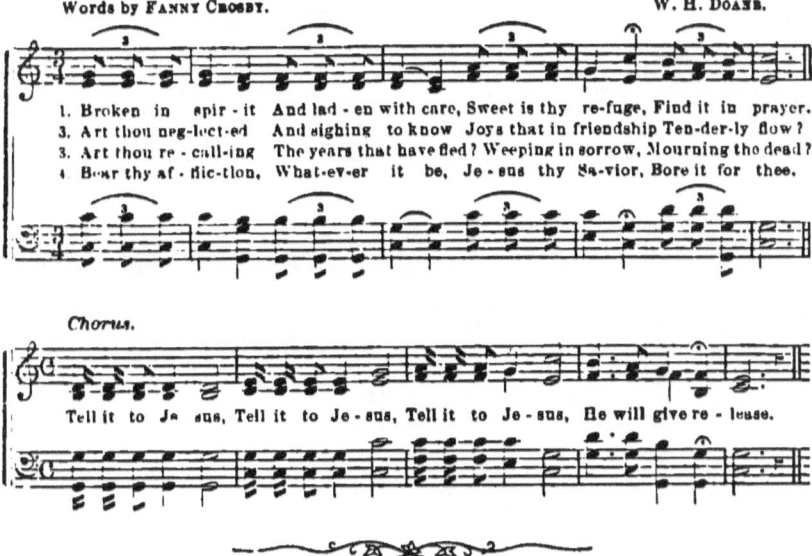

1. Broken in spir-it And lad-en with care, Sweet is thy re-fuge, Find it in prayer.
3. Art thou neg-lect-ed And sighing to know Joys that in friendship Ten-der-ly flow?
3. Art thou re-call-ing The years that have fled? Weeping in sorrow, Mourning the dead?
4. Bear thy af-flic-tion, What-ev-er it be, Je-sus thy Sa-vior, Bore it for thee.

Chorus.

Tell it to Je-sus, Tell it to Je-sus, Tell it to Je-sus, He will give re-lease.

BEAR THE CROSS.

Children's Chant.

Words by FANNY CROSBY. W. H. DOANE.

1. Bear the cross and follow...... | Je - sus, | Let his goodness............ | be our song;
2. Bear the cross, and live for... | Je - sus, | Tho' at times 't is............ | hard to bear;
3. Bear the cross without re-.... | pin - ing, | Joy will yet our............ | toil re - pay;
4. Bear the cross and work for.. | Je - sus, | Precious promise............ | he hath given;

If we falter he will............... | help us, | We are weak but............... | he is strong.
He will make the burden....... | light - er, | He will bear the............... | children's prayer.
Bear it with a cheerful.......... | spir - it, | Meekly bear it .... | day by day.
If we love him and are.......... | faith - ful, | Sweet will be our............... | rest in heaven.

NOTE.—By holding the first word of each line this Chant is rendered very effective.

JESUS GUIDE. Chant.

Words by JAMES UPHAM.

W. H. DOANE.

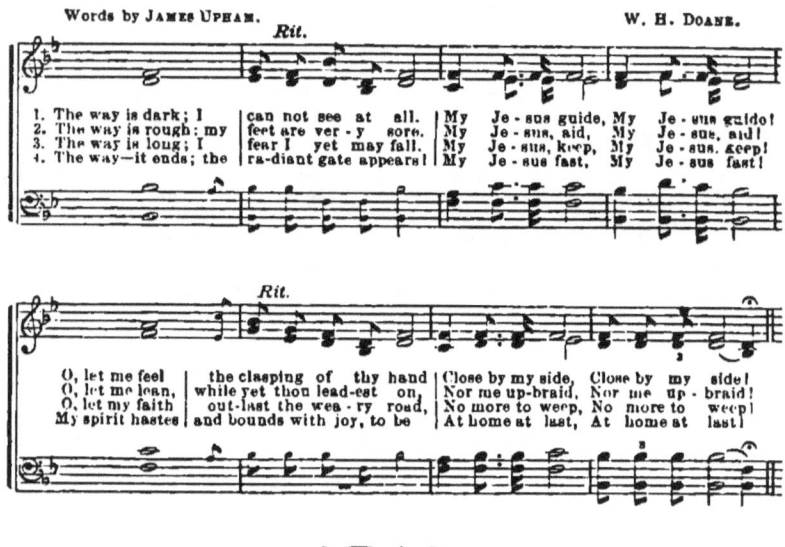

1. The way is dark; I | can not see at all. | My Je-sus guide, My Je-sus guide!
2. The way is rough: my | feet are ver-y sore. | My Je-sus, aid, My Je-sus, aid!
3. The way is long; I | fear I yet may fall. | My Je-sus, keep, My Je-sus, keep!
4. The way—it ends; the | ra-diant gate appears! | My Je-sus fast, My Je-sus fast!

O, let me feel | the clasping of thy hand | Close by my side, Close by my side!
O, let me lean, | while yet thou lead-est on, | Nor me up-braid, Nor me up-braid!
O, let my faith | out-last the wea-ry road, | No more to weep, No more to weep!
My spirit hastes | and bounds with joy, to be | At home at last, At home at last!

THE LORD IS MY SHEPHERD. Chant.

W. H. DOANE.

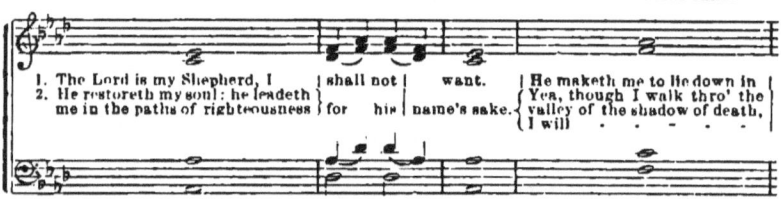

1. The Lord is my Shepherd, I | shall not | want. { He maketh me to lie down in
2. He restoreth my soul: he leadeth | | { Yea, though I walk thro' the
me in the paths of righteousness } for | his | name's sake. { valley of the shadow of death,
{ I will - - -

3. Thou preparest a table before | in }
the presence of mine enemies: thou } cup runneth | over. { Surely goodness and mercy
anointest my head with oil; my } { shall follow me - - - }

green pas | tures: | He leadeth me be- - | side the | still - - | waters
fear no | evil; | For thy rod and thy | staff they | com-fort | me.

all the | days of my life; | And I will dwell in the | house of the | Lord for- | ever.

JUST AS I AM. Chant.

W. H. Doane.

1. Just as I am, without one plea, But that thy blood was—shed for | me, {And that thou bidst me come to thee, O Lamb of—}God, I | come.

2 Just as I am, and waiting not To rid my soul of | one dark | blot,
To thee whose blood can cleanse each spot, O Lamb of | God I | come.

3 Just as I am, poor, wretched, blind, Sight, riches, healing | of the | mind,
Yea, all I seek in thee I find, O Lamb of | God I | come.

4 Just as I am, thy love unknown Has broken every | barrier | down;
Now to be thine, yea, thine alone, O Lamb of | God I | come.

THE OPEN GATE. Chant.

W. H. Doane.

1 Mercy with her wings unfolded, Bending o'er her | children | dear,
Softly whispers, "Come to Jesus, How he | loves your | praise to | hear."

2 With his gracious arms extended, See the kind Re- | deem-er | wait,
Now he folds the Lamb that enters, Joyful | through the | open | gate.

3 Shall we cling to earthly pleasure, When the shining | angels | wait,
Calling children to the Savior, Standing | at the | open | gate?

4 Joy the world can never give us, Pure, unfading | treasures | wait,
They who seek will surely find them, Find them | at the | open | gate.

I AM THE WAY. Chant.

W. H. Doane.

1 Art thou weary, art thou languid, Art thou | sore dis- | tressed?
"Come to me," saith One, and, coming, | Be at | rest.

2 Hath he marks to lead me to him, If he | be my | guide?
In his feet and hands are footprints, | And his | side.

3 Is there a diadem, as monarch, That his | brow a- | dorns?
Yes; a crown in very surety, | But of | thorns.

4 If I ask him to receive me, Will he | say me | nay?
No; not till earth, and not till heaven | Pass a- | way.

5 Finding, following, keeping, struggling, Is he | sure to | bless?
Angels, martyrs, prophets, virgins, | Answer, | Yes.

BESIDE THE CROSS. Chant.

W. H. DOANE.

1. Jews were wrought to cruel madness, | Christians fled in fear and sadness, · · |
2. At its foot her feet she planted, · · · | By the dreadful scene undaunted, · · |
3. Poets oft have sung her story, · · · · | Painters decked her brow with glory, · |

4. But no worship, song, or glory, · · · | Touches like that simple story, · · · |
5. And when under fierce oppression, · · | Goodness suffers like transgression, · · |
6. But if love be there, true-hearted, · · | By no grief or terror parted, · · · · |

Mary stood the · · · · · · · · · · · · · · | cross be- | side.
Till the gentle · · · · · · · · · · · · · · | suff' - rer | died.
Priests her name have · · · · · · · · · · | de - i- | fied.

Mary stood the · · · · · · · · · · · · · · | cross be- | side.
Christ again is · · · · · · · · · · · · · · | cru - ci- | fied.
Mary stands the · · · · · · · · · · · · · · | cross be- | side.

O GIVE THANKS. Chant.

Solo, or Semi-Chorus.   1st Response. Chorus.

1 O give thanks unto the Lord, for he is good;   Chorus. For his mercy endureth forever.
2 Give thanks unto the God of gods;   For his mercy endureth forever.
3 O give thanks unto the Lord of lords;   For his mercy endureth forever.
4 To him who alone doeth great wonders;   For his mercy endureth forever.
5 To him that by wisdom made the heavens;   For his mercy endureth forever.
6 To him that stretched out the earth above the waters; For his mercy endureth forever.

Solo, or Semi-Chorus.   2d Response. Chorus.   All.

A - men.

7 To him that made great lights;   Chorus. For his mercy endureth forever.
8 The sun to rule by day; the moon and stars to rule by
   night; · · · · · · · · · · · · · · · · · · ·   For his mercy endureth forever.
9 Who remembered us in our low estate;   For his mercy endureth forever.
10 And hath redeemed us from our enemies;   For his mercy endureth forever.
11 Who giveth food to all flesh;   For his mercy endureth forever.
12 O give thanks unto the God of heaven;   For his mercy endureth forever.

NOTE.—The Solos should be sung by the teachers, and the Responses by the scholars.

1   America.   6s & 4s.
Key G.

1 My country, 't is of thee,
  Sweet land of liberty,
    Of thee I sing;
  Land where my fathers died,
  Land of the pilgrim's pride,
  From every mountain side,
    Let freedom ring.

2 My native country! thee,
  Land of the noble free,
    Thy name I love;
  I love thy rocks and rills,
  Thy woods and templed hills;
  My heart with rapture thrills,
    Like that above.

3 Let music swell the breeze,
  And ring from all the trees
    Sweet freedom's songs:
  Let mortal tongues awake,
  Let all that breathe partake,
  Let rocks their silence break,
    The sound prolong.

4 Our fathers' God to thee,
  Author of liberty,
    To thee we sing;
  Long may our land be bright
  With freedom's holy light;
  Protect us by thy might,
    Great God, our King.

---

2   Lenox.   H. M.
Key B Flat.

1 Blow ye the trumpet, blow —
    The gladly solemn sound!
  Let all the nations know,
    To earth's remotest bound,
  The year of jubilee is come;
  The year of jubilee is come;
  Return, ye ransomed sinners home.

2 Exalt the Lamb of God,
    The sin-atoning Lamb;
  Redemption by his blood
    Through all the lands proclaim.
  The year of jubilee has come;
  Return, ye ransomed sinners, home.

3 Jesus, our great High Priest,
    Has full atonement made;
  Ye weary spirits, rest,
    Ye mournful souls be glad.
  The year of jubilee is come;
  Return, ye ransomed sinners, home.

---

3   Retreat.   L. M.
Key O.

1 From every stormy wind that blows,
  From every swelling tide of woes,
  There is a calm, a sure retreat;
  'T is found beneath the mercy-seat.

2 There is a place where Jesus sheds
  The oil of gladness on our heads;
  A place than all besides more sweet —
  It is the blood-bought mercy-seat.

3 There is a scene where spirits blend,
  Where friend holds fellowship with friend:
  Though sundered far, by faith they meet,
  Around one common mercy-seat.

4   Shepherd.   8s, 7s & 4s.
Key D.

1 Savior, like a Shepherd lead us,
  Much we need thy tenderest care;
  In thy pleasant pastures feed us,
  For our use thy folds prepare.
    Blessed Jesus, blessed Jesus,
  Thou hast bought us, thine we are,
    Blessed Jesus, blessed Jesus,
  Thou hast bought us, thine we are

2 We are thine, do thou befriend us,
  Be the Guardian of our way;
  Keep thy flock, from sin defend us,
  Seek us when we go astray.
    Blessed Jesus, blessed Jesus,
  Hear young children when they pray.

3 Thou hast promised to receive us,
  Poor and sinful though we be;
  Thou hast mercy to relieve us,
  Grace to cleanse, and power to free.
    Blessed Jesus, blessed Jesus,
  Let us early turn to thee.

4 Early let us seek thy favor,
  Early let us do thy will;
  Blessed Lord and only Savior
  With thy love our bosoms fill.
    Blessed Jesus, blessed Jesus,
  Thou hast loved us, love us still.

---

5   Sweet Hour of Prayer.
Key D.

1 Sweet hour of prayer! sweet hour of prayer!
  That calls me from a world of care,
  And bids me at my Father's throne,
  Make all my wants and wishes known;
  In seasons of distress and grief,
  My soul has often found relief,
  And oft escaped the tempter's snare,
  By thy return, sweet hour of prayer;
  And oft escaped the tempter's snare,
  By thy return, sweet hour of prayer.

2 Sweet hour of prayer! sweet hour of prayer!
  Thy wings shall my petition bear,
  To him whose truth and faithfulness,
  Engage the waiting soul to bless;
  And since he bids me seek his face,
  Believe his word, and trust his grace,
  I 'll cast on him my every care,
  And wait for thee, sweet hour of prayer.

3 Sweet hour of prayer! sweet hour of prayer!
  May I thy consolation share,
  Till from Mount Pisgah's lofty height,
  I view my home, and take my flight;
  This robe of flesh I 'll drop, and rise
  To seize the everlasting prize:
  And shout, while passing through the air,
  Farewell, farewell, sweet hour of prayer.

---

6   Coronation.   C. M.
Key G.

1 O for a thousand tongues to sing
  My great Redeemer's praise,
  The glories of my God and King,
  The triumphs of his grace.

2 Jesus — the name that charms our fears,
  That bids our sorrows cease;
  'T is music in the sinner's ears,
  'T is life and health and peace.

3 He breaks the power of canceled sin,
  He sets the prisoner free;
  His blood can make the foulest clean;
  His blood availed for me.

7　O, do not be discouraged.

Key G.

1 O, do not be discouraged,
　For Jesus is your Friend!
O, do not be discouraged,
　For Jesus is your Friend!
He will give you grace to conquer
He will give you grace to conquer
　And keep you to the end.

CHORUS.

I am glad I 'm in this army,
Yes, I 'm glad I 'm in this army,
Yes, I 'm glad I 'm in this army,
　And I 'll battle for the school.

2 Fight on, ye little soldiers,
　The battle you shall win,
Fight on, ye little soldiers,
　The battle you shall win;
For the Savior is your Captain,
For the Savior is your Captain,
　And he has vanquished sin.
　I am glad, etc.

3 And when the conflict 's over,
　Before him you shall stand,
And when the conflict 's over,
　Before him you shall stand.
You shall sing his praise forever,
You shall sing his praise forever,
　In Canaan's happy land.
　I am glad, etc.

8　Cross.　C. M.

Key B Flat.

1 Must Jesus bear the cross alone,
　And all the world go free?
No: there 's a cross for every one,
　And there is a cross for me.

2 How happy are the saints above
　Who once went sorrowing here;
But now they taste unmingled love,
　And joy without a tear.

3 The consecrated cross I 'll bear,
　Till death shall set me free,
And then go home my crown to wear,
　For there 's a crown for me.

9　Evening.　C. M.

Key A Flat.

1 In mercy, Lord, remember me,
　Through all the hours of night,
And grant to me most graciously
　The safeguard of thy might.

2 With cheerful heart I close mine eyes,
　Since thou wilt not remove;
O, in the morning let me rise
　Rejoicing in thy love.

3 Or, if this night should prove my last,
　And end my transient day's;
Lord take me to thy promised rest,
　Where I may sing thy praise.

10　Amboy.　6s & 4s.

Key F.

1 To-day the Savior calls:
　Ye wanderers come;
O, ye benighted souls,
　Why longer roam?

2 To-day the Savior calls;
　O, listen now!
Within these sacred walls
　To Jesus bow.

3 To-day the Savior calls
　For refuge fly;
The storm of justice falls,
　And death is nigh.

4 The Spirit calls to-day:
　Yield to his power;
O, grieve him not away!
　'T is mercy's hour.

11　Boylston.　S. M.

Key C.

1 Sow in the morn thy seed;
　At eve hold not thy hand,
To doubt and fear give thou no heed —
　Broadcast it o'er the land.

2 Thou know'st not which shall thrive —
　The late or early sown;
Grace keeps the precious germ alive,
　When and wherever strewn.

3 And duly shall appear,
　In verdure, beauty, strength,
The tender blade, the stalk, the ear,
　And the full corn at length.

4 Thou canst not toil in vain :
　Cold, heat, and moist, and dry,
Shall foster and mature the grain
　For garners in the sky.

12　St. Thomas.　S. M.

Key G.

1 I love thy kingdom, Lord—
　The house of thine abode—
The Church our blest Redeemer saved
　With his own precious blood.

2 I love thy Church, O God!
　Her walls before thee stand,
Dear as the apple of thine eye,
　And graven on thy hand.

3 For her my tears shall fall;
　For her my prayers ascend;
To her my cares and toils be given,
　Till toils and cares shall end.

4 Beyond my highest joy
　I prize her heavenly ways;
Her sweet communion, solemn vows
　Her hymns of love and praise.

5 Sure as thy truth shall last,
　To Zion shall be given
The brightest glories earth can y
　And brighter bliss of heaven.

13 Missionary Hymn. 7s & 6s.

Key F.

1 From Greenland's icy mountains,
From India's coral strand;
Where Afric's sunny fountains
Roll down their golden sand;
From many an ancient river,
From many a palmy plain,
They call us to deliver
Their land from error's chain.

2 What though the spicy breezes
Blow soft o'er Ceylon's isle;
Though every prospect pleases,
And only man is vile:
In vain with lavish kindness
The gifts of God are strewn;
The heathen in his blindness
Bows down to wood and stone.

3 Shall we, whose souls are lighted
With wisdom from on high,
Shall we to men benighted
The lamp of life deny?
Salvation—O salvation!
The joyful sound proclaim,
Till earth's remotest nation
Has learned Messiah's name.

4 Waft, waft, ye winds, his story,
And you, ye waters, roll,
Till, like a sea of glory,
It spreads from pole to pole;
Till o'er our ransomed nature
The Lamb for sinners slain,
Redeemer, King, Creator,
In bliss returns to reign.

14 America. 6s & 4s.

Key G.

1 God bless our native land!
Firm may she ever stand,
Through storm and night;
When the wild tempests rave
Ruler of winds and wave,
Do thou our country save
By thy great might.

2 For her our prayer shall rise
To God, above the skies;
On him we wait:
Thou who art ever nigh,
Guarding with watchful eye,
To thee aloud we cry,
God save the State!

15 Balerma. C. M.

Key B Flat.

O for a closer walk with God—
A calm and heavenly frame;
A light to shine upon the road
That leads me to the Lamb.

2 Where is the blessedness I knew,
When first I saw the Lord?
Where is the soul-refreshing view
Of Jesus and his word?

3 What peaceful hours I once enjoyed!
How sweet their memory still!
But they have left an aching void
The world can never fill.

4 Return, O holy Dove, return!
Sweet messenger of rest;
I hate the sins that made thee mourn,
And drove thee from my breast.

16 Arlington. C. M.

Key G.

1 There is a land of pure delight,
Where saints immortal reign;
Infinite day excludes the night,
And pleasures banish pain.

2 There everlasting spring abides,
And never with'ring flowers;
Death, like a narrow sea, divides
This heavenly land from ours.

3 Sweet fields beyond the swelling flood
Stand dressed in living green;
So to the Jews old Canaan stood,
While Jordan rolled between.

4 Could we but climb where Moses stood
And view the landscape o'er,
Not Jordan's stream, nor death's cold flood
Should fright us from the shore.

17 Laban. S. M.

Key D.

1 My soul, be on thy guard;
Ten thousand foes arise;
The hosts of sin are pressing hard
To draw thee from the skies.

2 O watch and fight and pray;
The battle ne'er give o'er;
Renew it boldly every day,
And help divine implore.

3 Ne'er think the victory won,
Nor lay thine armor down;
The work of faith will not be done
Till thou obtain the crown.

4 Then persevere till death
Shall bring thee to thy God;
He'll take thee, at thy parting breath,
To his divine abode.

18 Kindness. L. M.

Key A.

1 Awake, my soul, in joyful lays,
And sing thy great Redeemer's praise
He justly claims a song from me,
His loving kindness, O, how free!
His loving kindness, loving kindness,
His loving kindness, O, how free!

2 He saw me ruined by the fall,
Yet loved me, notwithstanding all;
He saved me from my lost estate,
His loving kindness, O, how great!

3 I often feel my sinful heart
Prone from my Savior to depart;
But though I oft have him forgot,
His loving kindness changes not.

4 Soon shall I pass the gloomy vale;
Soon all my mortal powers must fail;
O, may my last expiring breath
His loving kindness sing in death.

19   Webb.   7s & 6s.

Key B Flat.

1 The morning light is breaking,
   The darkness disappears;
The sons of earth are waking
   To penitential tears.
Each breeze that sweeps the ocean
   Brings tidings from afar,
Of nations in commotion,
   Prepared for Zion's war.

2 Rich dews of grace come o'er us
   In many a gentle shower,
And brighter scenes before us
   Are opening every hour.
Each cry, to heaven going,
   Abundant answers brings,
And heavenly gales are blowing,
   With peace upon their wings.

3 Blest river of salvation,
   Pursue thy onward way;
Flow thou to every nation,
   Nor in thy richness stay.
Stay not till all the lowly
   Triumphant reach their home;
Stay not till all the holy
   Proclaim—"The Lord is come!"

20   Weary.

Key C.

1 In the Christian's home in glory,
   There remains a land of rest;
There the Savior 's gone before me,
   To fulfill my soul's request.

CHORUS.

There is rest for the weary,
   There is rest for the weary,
There is rest for the weary,
   There is rest for you.
On the other side of Jordan,
   In the sweet fields of Eden,
Where the tree of life is blooming,
   There is rest for you.

2 He is fitting up my mansion,
   Which eternally shall stand,
For my stay shall not be transient
   In that holy, happy land.

3 Pain nor sickness ne'er shall enter,
   Grief nor woe my lot shall share;
But in that celestial center,
   I a crown of life shall wear.

4 Death itself shall then be vanquished,
   And his sting shall be withdrawn;
Shout for gladness, O, ye ransomed,
   Hail with joy the rising morn.

5 Sing, O, sing, ye heirs of glory;
   Shout your triumph as you go;
Zion's gate will open for you,
   You shall find an entrance through.

21   America.   6s & 4s.

Key G.

Come, thou Almighty King,
Help us thy name to sing,
   Help us to praise!
Father, all glorious,
O er all victorious,
Come and reign over us,
   Ancient of days.

2 God of the right, arise!
Scatter our enemies;
   Now make them fall!
Let thine almighty aid
Our sure defense be made,
Our souls on thee be stayed;
   Lord, hear our call!

3 Come, thou eternal Word,
Gird on thy mighty sword;
   Our prayer attend!
Come, and thy people bless,
Come, give thy word success;
Spirit of holiness
   On us descend!

22   Happy Day.   L. M.

Key G.

1 O happy day that fixed my choice
   On thee, my Savior and my God!
Well may this glowing heart rejoice,
   And tell its raptures all abroad.
   Happy day, happy day,
When Jesus washed my sins away;
He taught me how to watch and pray,
And live rejoicing every day.
   Happy day, happy day,
When Jesus washed my sins away.

2 O happy bond, that seals my vows
   To Him, who merits all my love;
Let cheerful anthems fill his house,
   While to that sacred shrine I move.

3 'T is done, the great transaction 's done,
   I am my Lord's, and he is mine;
He drew me, and I followed on,
   Charmed to confess the voice divine.

23   Hymn of Dedication.

TUNE—The Morning Light is Breaking.

MAIN SCHOOL.

Come join our dedication,
   While to our God we raise
Our thankful hearts' oblation,
   A hymn of grateful praise,
For all these blessings given,
   For this our Sabbath home,
Where we shall learn of heaven,
   And of the world to come.

BIBLE CLASSES.

We 'll join your dedication,
   And with you join to sing
A hymn of consecration,
   To God our Savior, King
Of all these pleasant places
   Where we shall learn his word,
And seek those Christian graces
   That make us like our Lord.

INFANT DEPARTMENT.

We 'll join the dedication,
   And sing as best we can
Big words that end in —*ation*,
   For sure we like the plan
Of this our pleasant quarter,
   And thank the great, good God,
Who taught our friends to alter
   And fix things for our good.

ALL.

Accept our dedication,
   Thou holy God above,
And grant us thy salvation
   And fill our hearts with love.
Here let thy Holy Spirit
   Upon our souls descend,
And make us all inherit
   The kingdom without end.

24   Dedication Hymn.

TUNE.—The Morning Light is Breaking.

1 To thee, O precious Savior,
   We dedicate this room ;
Come, ever blessed Spirit,
   I well in our Sabbath home!
Dwell in our hearts, dear Jesus!
   We give ourselves to thee ;
Wash us in blood atoning,
   Poured out ou Calvary.

2 Instruct us, heavenly Teacher!
   Thy sacred Word reveal,
And by thy grace assist us
   To do thy righteous will.
Guard all our steps, dear Savior!
   And on our pathway shine ;
Dispel all doubts and darkness,
   And make us wholly thine!

3 Thus train us in life's morning
   For service yet to come ;
To bear the cross with gladness,
   Till Thou shalt call us home.
Then when we meet in heaven,
   And join the blood-washed throng,
Redeeming love forever
   Shall be our joy and song.

25   Jesus Loves Me.

Key E Flat.

1 Jesus loves me! this I know,
   For the Bible tells me so :
Little ones to him belong ;
   They are weak, but he is strong.

CHORUS.

Yes, Jesus loves me ;
Yes, Jesus loves me ;
Yes, Jesus loves me,
   The Bible tells me so.

2 Jesus loves me! he who died,
   Heaven's gate to open wide ;
He will wash away my sin,
   Let his little child come in.

3 Jesus loves me! loves me still,
   Though I 'm very weak and ill ;
From his shining throne on high,
   Comes to watch me where I lie.

4 Jesus loves me! he will stay
   Close beside me all the way ;
If I love him when I die,
   He will take me home on high.

26   Battle Hymn of the Republic.

Key B Flat.

BY JULIA WARD HOWE.

1 Mine eyes have seen the glory of the coming of
   the Lord ;
He is tramping out the vintage where the
   grapes of wrath are stored ;
He hath loosed the fateful lightning of his ter-
   rible quick sword ;
   His truth is marching on.

2 I have seen him in the watch-fires of a hun-
   dred circling camps ;
They have builded Him an altar in the ev'ning
   dawn and damps ;
I have read his righteous sentence by the dim
   and flaring lamps :
   His day is marching on.

3 I have read a fiery gospel, writ in burnished
   rows of steel.
As ye deal with my contemners, so with you
   my grace shall deal ;
Let the Hero, born of woman, crush the ser-
   pent with his heel,
   Since God is marching on.

4 He has sounded forth the trumpet, that shall
   never call retreat,
He is sifting out the hearts of men before his
   judgment seat ;
O, be swift, my soul, to answer Him! be jubi-
   lant, my feet :
   Our God is marching on.

5 In the beauty of the lilies Christ was born
   across the sea,
With a glory in His bosom that transfigures
   you and me ;
As He died to make men holy, let us die to
   make men free,
   While God is marching on.

27   I Have a Father, &c.

Key E Flat.

1 I have a Father in the promised land,
I have a Father in the promised land,
   My Father calls me, I must go
To meet Him in the promised land,

CHORUS.

I'll away, I'll away to the promised land,
I'll away, I'll away to the promised land,
   My Father calls me, I must go
To meet Him in the promised land.

2 I have a Savior in the promised land,
I have a Savior in the promised land,
   My Savior calls me, I must go
To meet him in the promised land.
   CHO.—I'll away, I'll away to the, &c.

3 I have a crown in the promised land,
I have a crown in the promised land,
   When Jesus calls me, I must go
To wear it in the promised land.
   CHO.—I'll away, I'll away to the, &c.

28   I'm a Pilgrim.

Key G.

1 I'm a Pilgrim, and I'm a stranger ;
I can tarry, I can tarry but a night.
Do not detain me, for I am going
To where the fountains are ever flowing.
   I'm a pilgrim, and I'm a stranger,
   I can tarry, I can tarry but a night.

2 There the glory is ever shining :
I am longing, I am longing for the sight.
Here in this country so dark and dreary
I have been wandering, forlorn and weary.
   CHORUS—I'm a pilgrim, &c.

3 There's the city to which I journey,
My Redeemer, my Redeemer is its light ;
There is no sorrow, nor any sighing,
There is no sin there, nor any dying.
   CHORUS—I'm a pilgrim, &c.

29   Precious Name.

Key G.

1 There is no name so sweet on earth,
No name so sweet in heaven,
The name, before his wondrous birth,
To Christ, the Savior given.

REFRAIN.

We love to sing around our King,
And hail him blessed Jesus:
For there 's no word ear ever heard,
So dear, so sweet as Jesus.

2 His human name they did proclaim,
When Abram's son they sealed him,
The name that still, by God's good will,
Deliverer revealed him.

3 And when he hung upon the tree,
They wrote this name above him,
That all might see the reason we
For evermore must love him.

4 So now upon his Father's throne,
Almighty to release us
From sin and pains, he gladly reigns,
The Prince and Savior Jesus.

30   Rest. L. M.

Key D.

1 Asleep in Jesus! blessed sleep!
From which none ever wakes to weep;
A calm and undisturbed repose,
Unbroken by the last of foes.

2 Asleep in Jesus! O how sweet
To be for such a slumber meet!
With holy confidence to sing
That death hath lost its venomed sting.

3 Asleep in Jesus! O, for me
May such a blissful refuge be!
Securely shall my ashes lie,
And wait the summons from on high

31   We are out on the Ocean.

Key E Flat.

1 We are out on an ocean sailing;
Homeward bound we smoothly glide;
We are out on an ocean, sailing
To a home beyond the tide.

CHORUS.

All the storms will soon be over;
Then we 'll anchor in the harbor;
We are out on an ocean, sailing
To a home beyond the tide.

2 Millions now are safely landed
Over on the golden shore;
Millions more are on their journey,
Yet there 's room for millions more.
CHO.—All the storms, &c.

3 Come on board, oh, ship for glory,
Be in haste, make up your mind,
For our vessel 's weighing anchor,
And you may be left behind.
CHO.—All the storms, &c.

4 When we all are safely anchor'd,
We will shout our journey o'er,
We will walk about the city
And will sing for evermore.
CHO.—All the storms, &c.

32   The Sunday School.

Key G.

1 The Sunday School, that blessed place!
Oh, I would rather stay
Within its walls, a child of grace,
Than spend my hours in play,
The Sunday School, the Sunday School,
Oh, 'tis the place I love,
For there I learn the golden rule
Which leads to joys above.

2 'Tis there I learn that Jesus died
For sinners such as I;
Oh, what has all the world beside,
That I should prize so high?
The Sunday School, &c.

3 Then let our grateful tribute rise,
And songs of praise be given,
To Him who dwells above the skies,
For such a blessing given.
The Sunday School, &c.

4 And welcome, then, the Sunday School!
We'll read and sing, and pray,
That we may keep the golden rule,
And never from it stray.
The Sunday School.

33   Atonement. C. M.

Key B Flat.

1 There is a fountain filled with blood,
Drawn from Immanuel's veins:
And sinners, plunged beneath that flood,
Lose all their guilty stains.

2 The dying thief rejoiced to see
That fountain in his day;
And there may I, though vile as he,
Wash all my sins away.

3 Thou dying Lamb! thy precious blood
Shall never lose its power,
Till all the ransomed Church of God
Are saved, to sin no more.

4 Then in a nobler, sweeter song,
I 'll sing thy power to save,
When this poor lisping, stammering tongue
Lies silent in the grave.

34   Joyfully! Joyfully!

Key C.

4 Joyfully, joyfully, onward we move,
Bound to the land of bright spirits above:
Jesus, our Savior, in mercy says, Come,
Joyfully, joyfully, haste to your home.
Soon will our pilgrimage end here below,
Soon to the presence of God we shall go:
Then if to Jesus our hearts have been given,
Joyfully, joyfully, rest we in heaven.

2 Teachers and scholars have pass'd on before,
Waiting, they watch us approaching the shore
Singing to cheer us, while passing along,
Joyfully, joyfully, haste to your home.
Sounds of sweet music there ravish the ear,
Harps of the blessed, your strains we shall
hear,
Filling with harmony heaven's high dome,
Joyfully, joyfully, Jesus we come.

35 Around the Throne of God.

Key G.

1 Around the throne of God in heaven
Thousands of children stand,
Children whose sins are all forgiven,
A holy, happy band,
Singing glory, glory,
Glory be to God on high.

2 In flowing robes of spotless white
See every one array'd,
Dwelling in everlasting light,
And joys that never fade,
Singing glory, &c.

3 What brought them to that world above
That heaven so bright and fair,
Where all is peace, and joy, and love?
How came those children there?
Singing glory, &c.

36 Watchman, Tell us, &c.

Key D.

1 Watchman, tell us of the night,
What its signs of promise are,
Traveler, o'er you mountain's height,
See that glory beaming star!
Watchman, does its beauteous ray
Aught of hope or joy foretell?
Traveler, yes; it brings the day—
Promised day of Israel.

CHORUS.

Traveler, yes; it brings the day—
Promised day of Israel!

2 Watchman, tell us of the night,
Higher yet that star ascends;
Traveler, blessedness and light,
Peace and truth its course portends;
Watchman, will its beams alone
Gild the spot that gave them birth?
Traveler, ages are its own;
See, it bursts o'er all the earth!

CHORUS.

Traveler, ages are its own;
See, it bursts o'er all the earth!

3 Watchman, tell us of the night,
For the darkness seems to dawn,
Traveler, darkness takes its flight,
Doubt and terror are withdrawn.
Watchman, let thy wanderings cease;
Hie thee to thy quiet home:—
Traveler, lo! the Prince of Peace,
Lo! the Son of God is come.

CHORUS.

Traveler, lo! the Prince of Peace,
Lo! the Son of God is come.

37 Mary to the Savior's Tomb.

Key F.

1 Mary to the Savior's tomb
Hasted at the early dawn;
Spice she brought, and sweet perfume,
But the Lord she loved, had gone.
For awhile she lingering stood,
Fill'd with sorrow and surprise,
Trembling while a crystal flood
Issued from her weeping eyes.

2 But her sorrows quickly fled
When she heard his welcome voice:
Christ had risen from the dead;
Now he bids her heart rejoice:
What a change his word can make,
Turning darkness into day!
Ye who weep for Jesus' sake,
He will wipe your tears away.

38 Jesus paid it all.

Key G.

1 Nothing, either great or small,
Remains for me to do;
Jesus died, and paid it all,—
Yes, all the debt I owe.

CHORUS.

Jesus paid it all,
All the debt I owe,
Jesus died and paid it all,
Yes, all the debt I owe.

2 When he from his lofty throne
Stoop'd down to do and die,
Every thing was fully done,
"'Tis finish'd!" was his cry.
CHO.—Jesus paid it all, &c.

3 Weary, working, plodding one,
O, wherefore toil you so?
Cease your doing,—all was done,
Yes, ages long ago.
CHO.—Jesus paid it all, &c.

4 Till to Jesus' work you cling
Along by simple faith,
"Doing" is a deadly thing,
Your "doing" ends in death.
CHO.—Jesus paid it all, &c.

5 Cast your deadly "doing" down,
Down, all at Jesus' feet;
Stand in Him, in Him alone,
All glorious and complete.
CHO.—Jesus paid it all, &c.

39 Say, Brothers, will you meet us?

Key B Flat.

1 Say, brothers, will you meet us,
Say, brothers, will you meet us,
Say, brothers, will you meet us,
On Canaan's happy shore?

CHORUS.

Glory, glory, hallelujah,
Glory, glory, hallelujah,
Glory, glory, hallelujah,
For ever, evermore.

2 By the grace of God, we'll meet you,
By the grace of God, we'll meet you,
By the grace of God, we'll meet you,
On Canaan's happy shore.
CHO.—Glory, &c.

3 Jesus lives and reigns forever,
Jesus lives and reigns forever,
Jesus lives and reigns forever
On Canaan's happy shore.
CHO.—Glory, &c.

4 Glory in the highest glory,
Glory in the highest glory,
Glory in the highest glory,
On Canaan's happy shore.
CHO.—Glory, &c.

INDEX OF TUNES.

(158)

INDEX TO SUBJECTS.

NUMBERS INDICATE PAGES.

INDEX OF HYMNS—FIRST LINES.

—◦◦❀◦◦—

www.ingramcontent.com/pod-product-compliance
Lightning Source LLC
Chambersburg PA
CBHW021113020726
47500CB00003B/733